CAMBRIDGE SCHOOL CLASSICS PROJECT
CLASSICAL STUDIES 13-16

Book III. Pompey and Caesar

compiled from Plutarch, Suetonius and other ancient sources by
MARTIN FORREST, ERNEST HEATLEY, MIKE HUGHES
and MARGARET WIDDESS

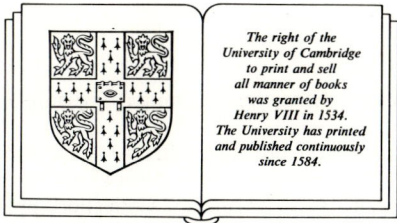

*The right of the
University of Cambridge
to print and sell
all manner of books
was granted by
Henry VIII in 1534.
The University has printed
and published continuously
since 1584.*

CAMBRIDGE UNIVERSITY PRESS
Cambridge
London   New York   New Rochelle
Melbourne   Sydney

Published by the Press Syndicate of the University of Cambridge
The Pitt Building, Trumpington Street, Cambridge CB2 1RP
32 East 57th Street, New York, NY 10022, USA
10 Stamford Road, Oakleigh, Melbourne 3166, Australia

This book, an outcome of work done for the Schools Council before its closure,
is published under the aegis of the School Curriculum Development Committee,
Newcombe House, 45 Notting Hill Gate, London W11 3JB.

First published 1986

Printed in Great Britain at the
University Press, Cambridge

ISBN 0 521 28699 9

DS

Acknowledgements

The authors and publisher would like to thank the following for permission to reproduce
illustrations:
The Ny Carlsberg Glyptotek, Copenhagen, front cover left, p 14l; Deutsches
Archäologisches Institut, Rome, front cover right, pp 21, 58b; Fitzwilliam Museum,
Cambridge, pp 6t, 9, 12, 55, 57b, 62, 63, 64; The Mansell Collection, pp 6b, 8, 11, 14r, 16,
18, 19, 20, 44; Robert Harding Associates, p 24t; Fototeca Unione, at the American
Academy in Rome, pp 24-5 (neg 5993F), 32 (negs 9094F, 4796F), 46 (neg 3341),
57t (neg 4799F), 58t (neg 13225F), 60b (neg 178); The Trustees of the British Museum,
pp 25l, r, 54; Cliché des Musées Nationaux, Paris, pp 28-9; Giraudon (in Musée des
Antiquités Nationales), p 35; Alinari, p 71b.
The publisher and authors ask for the forgiveness of those sources of illustrative material
whose identity it proved impossible to establish.
Maps and plan drawn by Reg Piggott.

Contents

Apart from the background material in chapter I, most of the text consists of ancient sources. This ancient source material is distinguished by larger type and an indication of the source. These abbreviated references are given alongside the source material in the left-hand margin, e.g. Plut. *Caes.* 1 means Plutarch's *Life of Caesar* chapter 1. Dates are given in the right-hand margin.

Features, which explain or amplify points in the material but do not form part of the continuous narrative, have a tinted background.

I The background

I.1 Rome

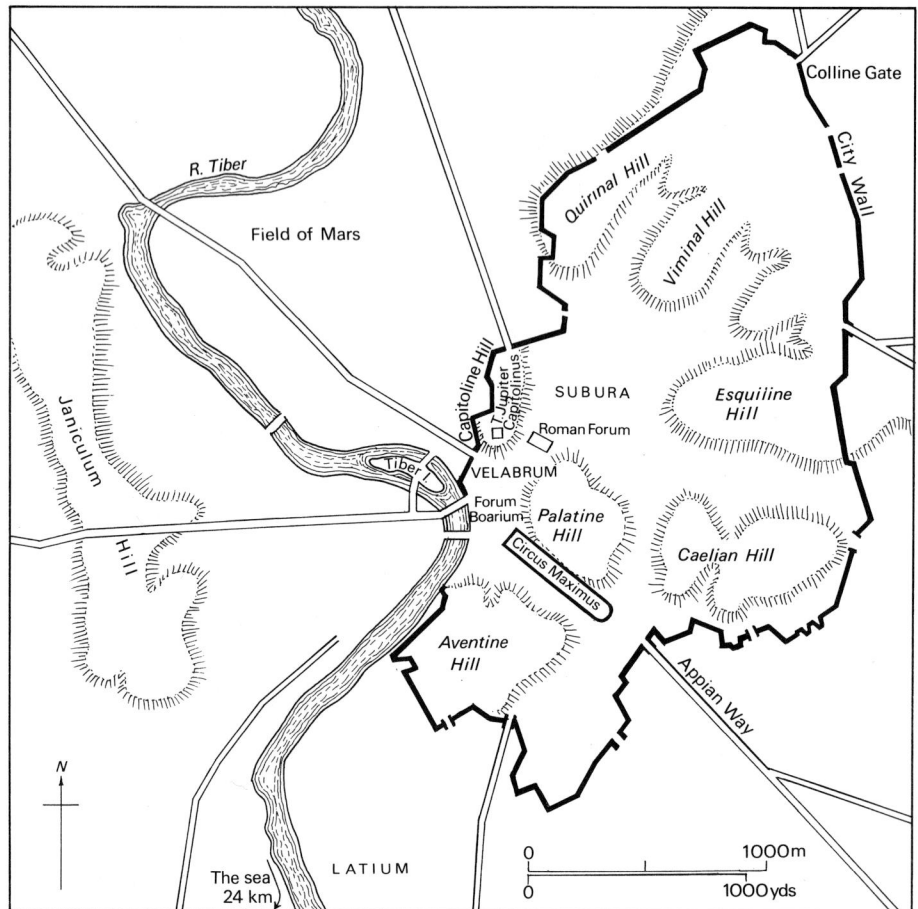

At the time of Caesar and Pompey, Rome had a population of about one million people. Of these, the vast majority lived in large blocks of apartments. Their problems were the same as those which have plagued city-dwellers for centuries – poor and cramped housing, lack of sanitation, noise, traffic, unemployment and poverty. The gulf between rich and poor was enormous, and there was no national health service or national insurance scheme to help the sick and unemployed. The rich, on the other hand, lived in large private houses and would often own several country estates and villas too. They also owned the apartment blocks in which the poor lived.

The heart of the city was the Forum, a low area of flat land between the Capitoline and Palatine hills. This was the political, legal and business centre of the city. Important citizens made their way there each day, followed by a crowd of 'clients' hoping for a small hand-out or perhaps an invitation to dinner – their reward for supporting their 'patron' and making him look important.   15

Near to the Forum was the noisy and crowded district known as the Subura. It was here in 100 B.C. that Julius Caesar was born, and here that he continued to live for the first 37 years of his life. His father was a man of some importance and had been governor of Asia, though he had never been elected to the highest position in the state, that of consul. All the same, some of Caesar's ancestors had been consuls and this was quite enough for the family to be regarded as noble.   20

Pompey also came from a noble family, though he was not born in Rome. He was six years older than Caesar and grew up in the area called Picenum where his father (a consul and a general) had built up a strong local following.   25

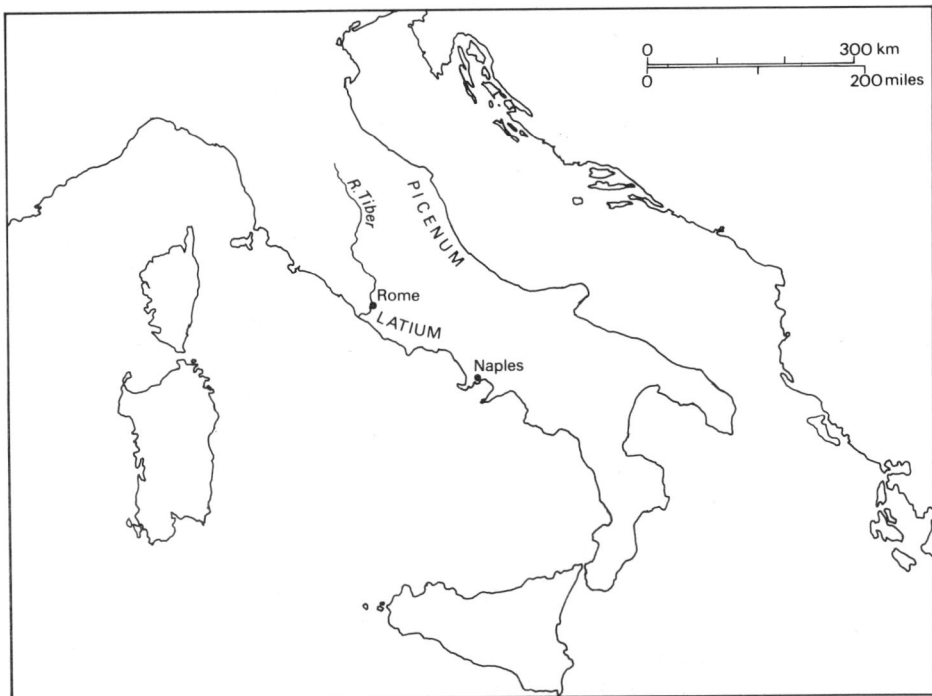

By the time of Caesar and Pompey, the Romans could look back over 600 years of history. Over that time, legends had grown up about their ancestors, both rich and poor, and about how the city was ruled long ago. Some of these stories were little more than fiction, whereas others contained a good deal of fact. Whatever the truth actually was, the stories do at least tell us the traditions which the Romans liked to believe and pass on to their children.   30

How Rome was ruled

Famous ancestors

Some Romans believed they were descended from the heroes of Troy, who had escaped to Italy when the Greeks captured their city.

ANCHISES = VENUS
|
AENEAS
(Trojan hero)
|
IULUS
|
ROMULUS
(the first king of Rome)

Rome becomes a Republic

According to the legends, there were seven kings, who ruled Rome for a total of nearly 250 years. The last king was a violent and arrogant man known as Tarquin the Proud. In 509 B.C. Tarquin was thrown out by a man named Brutus and the people set up a new form of government called the Republic. Each year they elected two *consuls* to be their leaders, and thus tried to make sure that never again would one man have all the power in Rome.

    This golden rule was only broken in times of crisis, when a *dictator* would be appointed to hold supreme power – but only until the crisis was over, and never for more than six months.

Symbols of power

Head of Venus on a coin issued by Julius Caesar in 47-46 B.C.

These men are called *lictors*. Twelve of them walked in front of each consul, carrying bundles of rods and axes known as 'fasces'. It was a tradition that if a consul wanted to make a speech, he would order the lictors to lower their fasces. This was a sign that the power of the consuls was in the hands of the people.

    Consuls and other government officials could also be recognised by their purple-edged togas.

5

10

15

The plebeians go on strike

In the early years of the Republic there were two distinct classes of people
in Rome, the patricians who had all the wealth and privileges, and the
plebeians who had none. Bad harvests forced many of the plebeians to   20
borrow from the patricians, but they were unable to pay back what they
owed. The laws about debt were harsh – imprisonment or slavery for those
who could not repay. The patricians kept promising to do something to
help the plebeians but they never did – so the plebeians went on strike and
left the city. There was panic amongst the patricians. What would happen,   25
they wondered, if someone took the opportunity to attack the city? It soon
became clear that they would have to reach a compromise with the
plebeians.

As a result, negotiations began which gave the plebeians the right to elect
two special officers to represent them. These officers were known as   30
tribunes of the people, and only plebeians were eligible. Each tribune had the
right of veto, which is Latin for 'I forbid'. It meant that a tribune could say
'veto' and forbid any law which seemed to be against the common people.
Tribunes could not be arrested and the people swore an oath to protect
them from intimidation. By the time of Caesar and Pompey, the number of   35
tribunes had risen to ten.

Over the years the position of the plebeians improved still further. The
decisions made in their assemblies were regarded as law, and some
plebeians rose to positions of wealth and importance.

Magistrates

Real power in Rome always remained in the hands of the wealthy – and   40
particularly in the hands of a small number of noble families. Each year the
elections were held and all the citizens met to vote. There were several
government officials to be chosen – the Romans called them all
'magistrates' – but none of them would receive any pay for their year of
office. This meant that all the magistrates came from the wealthy families   45
and the poor had few opportunities to play an important part in the
government.

Senators

After their year of office, all magistrates became members of a body known
as the *senate* – and remained members till the day of their death. In the
early days the senators had just been the king's advisers; in later times they 50
acquired great authority. Magistrates would change each year, but the
senate was always there. Its members were wealthy and experienced, so an
individual magistrate was unlikely to disagree with them. In any case, the
magistrate was soon to become a senator himself. The result was that
people came to rely on the senate and obeyed its decisions as if they were   55
laws.

I.2 Marius and Sulla

Little is known about the childhood of Caesar and Pompey, but we do know that they grew up at a time of great violence and bloodshed. Rome was by now a powerful city, controlling the whole of Italy and ruling parts of France, Spain, Africa, Greece and Asia Minor. There were wars at home and wars abroad, and the two leading figures of the day were the great generals, Marius and Sulla. 5

Stone sarcophagus (coffin) showing various stages of childhood.

Marius' mules

Rome was involved in a war in Africa. It was not going well and the people were annoyed with the senate for appointing such feeble generals. In 107 B.C. a man named Marius was elected consul, even though he did not come from a wealthy and noble family. Then the people gave him the command in Africa. 10

Up to this time the army had consisted of part-time 'soldier-citizens'. Marius changed it into a full-time professional body, with proper training and proper equipment. The amount of equipment carried by the soldiers gave them their nickname – 'Marius' mules'. Each of these soldiers swore an oath of loyalty to his general; in return, he expected him to provide fair pay and a hand-out from the booty captured in war. In some cases soldiers were provided with a plot of land at the end of their service. 15

The new army was very successful in Africa. Marius became so popular that when Italy was threatened by tribes invading from the north, he was elected consul for five successive years from 104 to 100 B.C. Again the new army proved its worth. 20

War with the Italian allies

Another change involved Rome's allies in Italy. These allies had served Rome well and wanted to become citizens of Rome. For some time their requests had been refused, so in 90 B.C. they rebelled. They scored some early successes and, despite some bitter fighting, Rome was forced into meeting their demands. 25

Sulla marches on Rome

One of Marius' own commanders now began to challenge his authority. His name was Sulla and he had already proved himself an able soldier in the wars in Africa. Sulla was consul in 88 B.C. and the senate decided to give him an important command in the East, fighting in the war against King Mithridates. It was a command which Marius dearly wanted, and he got it for himself by persuading the people to overrule the senate's decision.

Sulla was not the sort of man to stand for this. His army, which had recently been fighting in the war with the Italian allies, marched on Rome. It was the first time that a Roman had led an army against his own city. Marius had to escape and went to join some of his veteran soldiers in Africa. In this way Sulla forced the people into giving him back his command and he set off for the East.

Marius and Cinna

As soon as Sulla was gone, Marius came back from Africa and marched on Rome. He joined forces with Cinna, a consul the senate had tried to remove. They organised the massacre of their opponents. There were no elections. They declared themselves consuls for the following year, 86 B.C.

In this way Marius began his seventh consulship; but by now he was ill and exhausted. His death, seventeen days later, left Cinna in complete control of Rome. The next two years were relatively peaceful, but all the time Rome was waiting for the return of Sulla. It was an event which Cinna never saw. He was prepared to cross the seas and fight Sulla, but his soldiers mutinied and Cinna was killed.

Sulla becomes dictator

In 83 B.C. Sulla returned to Italy after a successful war in the East. He marched on Rome and captured it. 70,000 surviving supporters of Marius attacked him, but they were defeated in a grim battle outside the Colline gate.

A law was now passed in the assembly of the people which revived the ancient office of dictator and gave it to Sulla. This dictatorship, however, was very different from those of the past because it was Sulla who was to decide when he should resign.

He now organised Rome so that the senate should have almost complete power and the people very little. He put the senate in charge of the courts and took away the power of the tribunes. He was worried that supporters of Marius might persuade the people to revolt against the senate, so he gave orders that a list of names should be set up in the forum. It was a list of all those who had supported Marius. He declared that if a man's name appeared on that list he was an outlaw. A large reward would be paid to anyone who brought in the head of an outlawed man – even to a slave who had killed his master or to a son who had killed his father. These lists were put up not only in Rome, but in every city in Italy. New names were added every day as people were falsely accused of being supporters of Marius.

Portrait of Sulla on a coin issued about 25 years after his death. Cos. is an abbreviation of consul.

30

35

40

45

50

82 B.C.

55

60

65

II The early careers of Caesar and Pompey

From this point on the lives of Caesar and Pompey will be told through the words of the Greeks and Romans themselves.

To begin with, their careers were quite separate, so Chapter II follows first the early career of Caesar (100 B.C. – 67 B.C.) and then goes back to trace the early career of Pompey (106 B.C. – 66 B.C.).

II.1 Gaius Julius Caesar

Caesar was eighteen when Sulla became dictator. He had not yet joined the army, nor begun any career in politics – but Sulla had other reasons for keeping a close watch on him.

Plut.
Caes. 1 Caesar's wife was called Cornelia. She was the daughter of Cinna, who had once been the sole ruler of Rome. When Sulla came to power he tried to 5 make Caesar divorce her, but neither promises nor threats could persuade him. In the end Sulla confiscated Cornelia's dowry. Caesar was also the nephew of Marius and this was the main reason why he hated Sulla.

In the early days, Sulla had been busy with so many murders that he had overlooked Caesar. But Caesar was not content with this and entered the 10 elections as a candidate for the priesthood – even though he was still only a boy. Sulla did not oppose him openly; but secretly he made sure that Caesar did not get the priesthood. He also discussed the question of having Caesar removed. When his advisers said that there was no point in killing a boy like him, Sulla replied 'Have you no sense? Can't you see that in this 15 boy there are many Mariuses?'

An escape and a capture   81 B.C.

When Caesar got to hear of this he hid himself for some time, wandering from place to place in the district of the Sabines. He became ill and one night, while he was going from one house to another, he fell into the hands of Sulla's soldiers. They were searching the area to arrest people in hiding 20 and Caesar only escaped by bribing their leader to let him go.

Immediately, he left for the sea shore and set sail for Asia. Having spent some time there, he set out on a voyage back, but was captured by the pirates who controlled the sea with their huge fleets of ships.

At first the pirates demanded a ransom of twenty talents. Caesar laughed 25 at them and said, 'You don't seem to realise what an important man you've captured. I suggest you ask for fifty talents.'

Then he sent his companions to various cities to raise the money. He was left amongst the pirates with only one friend and two slaves. The pirates were Cilicians and most bloodthirsty murderers, but he treated them with 30 such contempt that whenever he lay down to sleep he would send a slave to tell them to stop talking. For thirty-eight days he treated them as though they were his private army, not his kidnappers. He took part in all their games and exercises without seeming at all concerned. He even wrote poems and speeches and read them out loud to the pirates. If they did not 35

Pirates

Plut.
Pomp. 24

While the Romans had been occupied with the wars between Sulla and
Marius, the power of the pirates had grown. Their main lair was in Cilicia.
They no longer attacked only seafarers, but began to devastate islands and
coastal cities too. It was not long before rich and powerful men of famous
families and great intelligence turned to piracy. They were attracted by the
glamour of it all. They built fortified harbours and signal beacons for the
use of their ships. They had fleets of light and nimble vessels with powerful
crews and skilful navigators. But far more annoying than the fear caused
was the luxury of their way of life – their sails embroidered with gold, their
purple sunshades, their oars clad in silver – as if their life were one riotous
party. Every coast echoed to the sound of their pipes and lyres and
drunken festivals. They kidnapped men of high importance and held
captured cities to ransom.

All this was a dreadful insult to the power of Rome. In fact they insulted
the Romans more than anyone else. They would leave their ships on the
shore and go plundering along the Roman roads sacking the villas on either
side. Once they actually captured two officials dressed in their purple-
edged togas and carried them off along with their attendants and lictors.

But this was their biggest insult; if they captured a man and he claimed
to be a Roman citizen and gave his name, they would all pretend to be
frightened out of their wits. They would smack their thighs and throw
themselves down before him begging him to pardon them. Seeing them so
humble and grovelling the Roman would be completely fooled and believe
them. One of the pirates would put a pair of Roman boots upon his feet
while others draped a toga over his shoulders, saying that this was to
prevent anyone making the same mistake again. So, for a long time they
would make fun of their prisoner and enjoy themselves at his expense. In
the end when they had reached the open sea, they would let down a ladder
over the side of the ship and invite him to return to land with no hard
feelings. If he was not keen to leave they would push him overboard
themselves and drown him.

Figures in togas.

like anything he had written he called them 'uneducated barbarians'. Often he would laugh and say that he would hang them all. The pirates were delighted with all this. They thought he was so outspoken because he was young and carefree.

Eventually his ransom money arrived from Miletus. He paid it over and was set free. As soon as he reached Miletus he manned some ships and set sail from the harbour to find the pirates again. He caught them with their ships still lying at anchor and he took most of them prisoner. He kept their treasures for himself and locked his captives in the prison house at Pergamum. Then he went in person to Junius the governor of Asia and told him that it was his duty to punish the prisoners. But Junius kept eyeing the treasure and saying he needed a bit more time to think the matter over. In the end, Caesar decided he was wasting his time with Junius and returned to Pergamum. He took the pirates out of prison and crucified them all, as he had often jokingly promised he would. 50

40

45

II.2 The start of Caesar's career

It was while he was in Asia that Caesar first saw military service. He served under 80 B.C. two Roman governors and once won the oak-leaf crown for saving the life of a fellow-soldier. He also went to the island of Rhodes to study the art of public 75 B.C. speaking. Caesar had great natural talent as a political speaker and worked hard to develop this ability. 5

In 69 B.C. Caesar's aunt Julia and his wife Cornelia both died.

Suet. Caes. 6, 7 Caesar made the usual speech from the rostra in praise of his aunt and it contained the following words:

> 'My aunt Julia is descended both from the kings and from the immortal
> gods. On her mother's side, the family name 'Marcii Reges' comes from 10
> King Ancus Marcius. On her father's side, the Julii are descended from
> Venus. So our family is as sacred as the kings and as holy as the gods.'

After the funeral, Caesar was sent to serve as quaestor in Further Spain. 68 B.C. There he was a travelling judge, going from town to town with the governor's authority. Once he came to Gades and noticed a statue of 15 Alexander the Great in the temple of Hercules. He heaved a sigh when he saw it; he seemed annoyed that he had achieved so little of note at an age when Alexander had already conquered the whole world. He immediately asked for his discharge, so that he could go and seize the first opportunity to make a name for himself in Rome. 20

It was about this time that Caesar remarried. His new wife was Pompeia, who was one of Sulla's granddaughters.

Meanwhile the pirate problem was on the increase. The year in which Caesar 67 B.C. returned to Rome saw the matter come to a head.

Plut. *Pomp.* 25 The power of the pirates spread over the whole of our sea, so that it was 25 impossible for ships to sail and merchants to do business. There were almost no goods for sale in the markets and great shortages were expected. The people at Rome began to say that someone should be sent out to rid the sea of pirates, and the man suggested for the task was Pompey the Great.

Coin issued by Caesar in 47-46 B.C. showing Aeneas, father of Iulus, escaping from Troy. He carries his own father on his back and holds a sacred statue of Minerva (Athene).

The road to success

Family

The best start in life was to be born into a family with ancestors who had been consuls. Such families were called *nobiles* – a name which originally meant well-known or famous. These families were the most influential, but it was not impossible for outsiders to make it to the top. These outsiders were called 'new men' and Cicero is probably the most famous example of a new man who attained the consulship. Marius was also a 'new man'.

5

Education

Rome had no state education system, and parents paid for their children's education directly. Studies in literature and philosophy were an important background for the study of law and oratory – the art of speaking in public.

A spell in the army was also considered an essential training for those who wanted to succeed.

10

Politics

All government officials were called magistrates and they were elected by the people. They were unpaid and held office for one year. The magistracies had to be held in a strict order which Sulla had reinforced. 'He forbade anybody to hold the office of praetor until he had held that of quaestor, or to be consul before he had been praetor.' (Appian)

15

Minimum age	Title	Responsibilities	Number elected	Notes
30	quaestor	2 in charge of treasury in Rome. Others assisted the governors of provinces.	20	All quaestors automatically became senators.
37	*aedile	Streets, traffic, water supply, markets, corn supply, building regulations, public games.	4	Not an essential step.
40	praetor	Administration of justice.	8	Could become provincial governor in the following year.
43	consul	Supreme magistrate in all matters of peace and war.	2	Could become provincial governor in following year.

*An alternative to becoming aedile was to become tribune. Only plebeians were eligible and ten were elected each year. They had the right of veto against any act of the senate or other magistrates. They could summon assemblies of the plebeians, and decisions made in these assemblies became law.

II.3 Pompey the Great

Pompey was the obvious man for the command against the pirates, as Plutarch's account of his earlier career explains.

His character and appearance

Plut. *Pomp.* 1-2

There were many reasons why Pompey was so popular and so loved. He lived modestly, trained hard for battle and spoke persuasively; he was trusted by others and found it easy to get on with them. From the beginning he had the sort of looks that made him popular with the people and won them over even before he started speaking.

5

Head of Pompey the Great (about 50 B.C.).

Pompey and Alexander

Pompey's hair stood up in a slight wave at the front and his face had an easy, appealing look – especially around the eyes. People said that he looked like the statues of King Alexander, but the resemblance was not very close. He was often called Alexander in his early years, and Pompey did not seem to mind the name.

Plut. *Pomp.* 2

Bust of Alexander the Great. (Roman copy of Greek original).

Two marriages

Shortly after his father's death, Pompey was accused of the theft of public property. (His father had given him some war booty, but it had later been stolen from Pompey.)

87 B.C.

10

Plut. *Pomp.* 4

The trial began with many exchanges between Pompey and his accuser. Pompey had a quick mind and was much more confident than most people of his age. This so impressed Antistius, the praetor who was judging the case, that he became very fond of Pompey and offered him his daughter in marriage. Pompey accepted his offer and the engagement was made in secret. All the same, most people knew what was going on because Antistius was so keen on Pompey. At the end of the trial, Antistius announced that the judges' verdict was 'Not Guilty'. It was like a signal to the crowd and they all shouted out 'Talasio' – the word which is traditionally shouted at weddings.

15

20

It was four years later that Sulla returned from the East and marched on Rome. 83 B.C.
Pompey was only twenty-three at the time, but he managed to raise an army to
support Sulla.

Plut.
Pomp. 9 When Sulla became dictator, he rewarded all of his generals. He was
impressed with the qualities of Pompey and thought that he would be very 25
useful to him. So he was keen to form some connection with Pompey
through marriage. His wife Metella also liked the idea, so they persuaded
Pompey to divorce Antistia and marry Aemilia, who was Metella's
daughter by a previous marriage. Aemilia too was already married and was
even pregnant at the time. 30

The whole arrangement was typical of a tyranny. It was not to Pompey's
liking, but it suited the needs of Sulla. In fact it turned out to be a year of
tragedy. Antistia's father had died early in the year, murdered by an enemy
of Pompey and Sulla. Next her mother committed suicide after seeing all
that had happened. Finally Aemilia died in childbirth, shortly after going 35
to live with Pompey.

Two triumphs

Sulla next sent Pompey to fight in Africa. He was so successful and so popular that
Sulla gave him the title 'Magnus' – the Great. 80 B.C.

Plut.
Pomp. 14 After this, Pompey asked permission to hold a triumphal procession, but
Sulla refused. He said that the law only allowed a praetor or a consul to 40
hold a triumph. Pompey was only just old enough to grow a beard. What
would people think of a triumph for a man who was too young for the
senate? They would not like such an honour and they would not like Sulla's
government.

But Pompey did not give up. He told Sulla to remember that more 45
people worship the rising sun than the setting sun. Sulla did not hear the
words clearly, but he could see that those who did were amazed. He asked
them what had been said. When he found out, he was astounded at
Pompey's boldness. Then he twice shouted out 'Let him have his
triumph'. 50

After Sulla's death Pompey supported the senate, campaigning first in Italy and 77-71
Gaul, and then in Spain. After a struggle, opposition was wiped out and Pompey's B.C.
reputation was further increased.

Meanwhile Spartacus and his gladiators had escaped from their barracks and
were leading a rebellion of Italian slaves. When Pompey returned to Italy, he found 71
that the slave rebellion was at its height. B.C.

Plut.
Pomp. 21 Crassus was the Roman commander against the slaves. When he learned of
Pompey's return, he decided to lead his army into a sudden and dangerous
battle. He was successful and killed 12,300 of the enemy. Even so, Fortuna
managed to give Pompey a share of the success; for 5,000 fugitives from the 60
battle ran into Pompey's army and were all killed. Pompey outdid Crassus

15

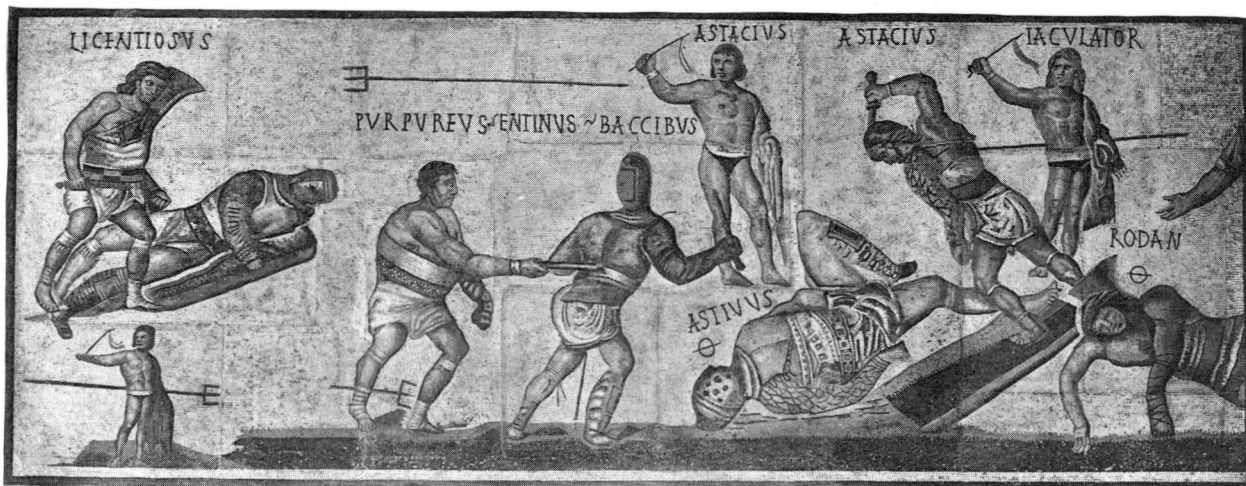

LICENTIOSVS   PVRPVREVS ENTINVS ~ BACCIBVS   ASTACIVS   ASTACIVS   IACVLATOR   RODAN   ASTIVVS

Mosaic showing life-size figures of different gladiators. (4th century A.D.)

by writing to the senate that Crassus had defeated the gladiators in pitched battle, but that he himself had stamped out the rebellion completely.

There was a fear that Pompey would not disband his army but would aim for a position like Sulla's, using armed force and having absolute power. But Pompey removed these suspicions and announced that he would disband his army after his triumph. So he was voted his second triumph and then the consulship.

The consulship

Plut.
Pomp. 22 Crassus also wanted to be consul. He was the richest politician of his time, the ablest speaker and the greatest man. He looked down on Pompey and on everyone else. All the same, he did not dare to enter the elections until he had begged for Pompey's support. Pompey was delighted to help him, but after they had been elected they disagreed on all points and were always arguing.

Crassus was the stronger of the two in the senate, but Pompey had great power with the people and gave them back their tribunes.

65

70

75

70 B.C.

II.4   Action against the pirates

Plut.
Pomp. 25 The tribune Gabinius now proposed a law which would give Pompey not just command of the navy, but power over all men, indeed the power of a king. For this law would give him control over all the sea on this side of the pillars of Hercules, and over all land to a distance of 50 miles (80 km) inland from the shore. This meant, in fact, that he would have power over every country which was under Roman rule, over the greatest nations and the mightiest kings. He was to choose 15 captains from the senate and to

67 B.C.

5

take as much money as he wanted from the public treasury. He was to have 200 ships and the right to levy as many soldiers and oarsmen as he wanted.

When these proposals were read out from the rostra the common people were absolutely delighted, but the most important and powerful senators thought that such unlimited power was frightening and so they all opposed the law – except for Caesar. He supported it. This was not because he cared about Pompey, but because he was always trying to make himself popular with the common people.

Plut. *Pomp.* 26
When the time came for the vote to be taken on this law, Pompey slipped off into the countryside for the day. When he heard that the law had been passed, he came back into the city in the darkness of night. He did this because he felt that if the people came pouring out in crowds to meet him it might make him some jealous enemies.

On the next day he came out in public and offered up a sacrifice. An assembly of the people was called and he managed to get from them many more things than had been mentioned in the law – in fact his force was made nearly twice as big. He was given 500 ships, 120,000 heavy-armed foot-soldiers, 5,000 cavalrymen, 24 captains and 2 quaestors. The price of goods suddenly fell and the people were jubilant, saying that the very name of Pompey had ended the war.

With tireless energy and the eager support of his officers Pompey cleared all the western seas of pirates within forty days. Plutarch says that he sent those who escaped 'buzzing back to their hive in Cilicia'.

Plut. *Pomp.* 27
Some of the pirate gangs who were still roving the seas begged Pompey for mercy. He treated them kindly and, apart from confiscating their ships and making them his captives, he did them no harm. Seeing this, other pirates began to hope for mercy too. They slipped away from their captains and fled with their wives and children to Pompey. He spared them all and it was mainly with their help that he was able to track down and deal with those who still lurked in their hiding-places, refusing to give themselves up because they knew their crimes were unpardonable. These were the most

Plut. *Pomp.* 28
powerful pirates. They lodged their families and treasure and all their useless people in forts and strong castles near the Taurus mountains and waited for Pompey's attack off the coast of Cilicia. He defeated them in a sea battle and then laid siege to their strongholds until, in the end, they begged for mercy and surrendered themselves and their cities and the islands which they controlled.

Within three months the war was finished and piracy swept from the sea. As well as many other vessels, the pirates surrendered 90 ships with bronze beaks and Pompey captured over 20,000 men. He had no wish to kill them all, but he knew it would be bad to let them go as there were so many of them and they were so uncivilised and warlike. On the other hand, he thought even wild animals become tame when they are treated kindly. So he decided to take the pirates away from the sea and give them homes and land, and to let them have a taste of the gentle life by living in cities and tilling the soil.

II.5 A new command

Mithridates wearing a lion skin. This is an imitation of the statues Alexander the Great had made.

Before he could return to Rome, news came to Pompey that the tribune Manilius had proposed a law to give him command over all the Roman armies of Asia, with orders to wage war there against King Mithridates. The aristocrats were not happy about giving Pompey so much power; they thought it was like setting up a tyranny. In private they encouraged each other to oppose the law and not to give up their freedom. But when the time came, their hearts failed them because they were afraid of the people.

The law was passed and Pompey in his absence was given almost all the powers which Sulla had got by attacking the city with armed forces.

66 B.C.

5

10

15

20

Summary of the early careers of Caesar and Pompey

CAESAR	B.C.	POMPEY
	106	Born.
Born.	100	
Nominated to become priest of Jupiter.	87	On trial for theft of war booty. Marries Antistia.
Marries Cornelia.	84	
	83	Raises army to support Sulla.
Escapes from Sulla.	81	Marries Aemilia.
Military service in Asia.	80	Fights in Africa. Given title of 'Magnus'.
Captured by pirates. Studies in Rhodes.	75	
	71	Helps to end slave rebellion.
	70	Consul with Crassus.
Deaths of aunt (Julia) and wife (Cornelia).	69	
Quaestor in Spain.	68	
Returns to Rome. Marries Pompeia.	67	Command against pirates.
Curator of Appian Way.	66	Command against Mithridates.

III   From 66 B.C. to the start of the civil war

III.1   Spend, spend, spend

Caesar meanwhile continued his career in politics. While all the debates had been
going on about Pompey's commands, Caesar had been appointed curator of the
Appian Way. This was the oldest Roman road of all and its remains are still to be
seen for many miles south of Rome. Plutarch tells us that Caesar spent not only
the official allowance but vast sums of his own money on the repair of the road.   5

The Appian Way. The circular building is the tomb of Caecilia Metella, who was married to one of Caesar's officers. (In the thirteenth century the tomb was converted into the keep of a castle.)

In 65 B.C. Caesar took the next major step up the ladder by becoming aedile.

Suet.
Caes. 10

As aedile, Caesar put on shows for the people – wild beast hunts and stage
plays.
    He paid for some of these out of his own pocket and shared the cost of
the rest with his colleague, Marcus Bibulus. In fact it was Caesar who got   10
all the credit, whether they had shared the cost or not.
    Caesar also provided a display of gladiators – but he did not have as
many pairs fighting as he wanted, for his enemies were terrified to see what
a gang of men he had collected. (Caesar had gathered together 320 pairs of
gladiators.) So the senate met specially to pass a law limiting the number of   15
gladiators anyone could keep in the city.

Plut.
Caes. 5

    By doing all this and by spending huge amounts on processions and
public banquets Caesar put to shame the efforts of every aedile before him.
The people were so delighted that everyone was looking for new offices and
honours to heap upon him.   20

Plut.
Caes. 4

    At first his enemies thought that his popularity would vanish as soon as
he stopped spending money; so they did nothing, while all the time he was
becoming more and more popular with the people. Later, when it was too
late to do anything about it, they realised that Caesar was making himself
popular for one reason only – so that he could destroy the Republic.   25

The face of Marius

Plut.
Caes. 6 In the city there were two groups – the supporters of Sulla, who had held power since Sulla died, and the supporters of Marius, who were downtrodden, scattered and frightened to show themselves. Caesar wanted to reorganise the supporters of Marius and become their leader. While he was aedile and in the middle of his great displays, he had statues of Marius made secretly and also statues of the goddess Victory carrying trophies. He gave orders that they should be set up on the Capitol by night. 30

At dawn next day, when the people saw the statues all beautifully made and glittering with gold, they were amazed at Caesar's courage in setting them up (for they guessed it was Caesar who had done it). Word of what had happened spread quickly and people crowded in to see for themselves. Some of them started shouting against Caesar and said that he was trying to use the people to make himself the sole ruler of Rome. But the supporters of Marius began to encourage each other and suddenly came out into the open in surprising numbers and the Capitol was filled with the racket of their applause. Tears of joy came to the eyes of many of them when they saw once again the face of Marius and they were full of praise for Caesar. 35 40

Pontifex Maximus

Remains of the Temple of Vesta, reconstructed from the ruins in 1930. Near it stood the Regia and the House of the Vestal Virgins.

The Pontifex Maximus was Rome's chief priest. His duties included supervision of the Vestal Virgins, whose job it was to keep the eternal fire burning in the Temple of Vesta. He also supervised the priests who were responsible for the worship of particular gods and goddesses. 45 50 55

Plut. *Caes.* 7 and Suet. *Caes.* 13 At about this time the Pontifex Maximus died and Caesar announced that he would stand as a candidate for the post. There was fierce competition and Caesar spent large sums of money on bribery. On the day of the

election Caesar's mother came to the door with him; there were tears in her 60
eyes. Caesar kissed her goodbye and said 'Today, Mother, your son will
either become Pontifex Maximus or an exile'.

The result of the election was that Caesar won by a huge majority, 63 B.C.
defeating two candidates who were older and higher-ranking than he was.

Suet.
Caes. 46 At first he lived in the Subura in an ordinary sort of house, but after he 65
was elected Pontifex Maximus he went to live in the Regia in the Sacred
Way.

Caesar's appearance and character

Suet.
Caes. 45 Caesar was rather fussy about his appearance. He was very particular about
how the barber cut his hair and shaved him, and some say that he used to
have the hair on other parts of his body plucked. He was bald and this used
to make him very embarrassed, especially since his enemies were always
making jokes about it. He used to comb forward the few hairs he had, and, 5
of all the honours which the senate and people later voted him, he was most
pleased with the right to wear a laurel wreath at all times! He is said to have
worn unusual clothes too. He wore a senator's tunic with the usual purple
stripe but with fringes hanging down at the wrists. He wore it loosely
hitched up with a belt and Sulla often used to warn the nobles to keep an 10
eye on the 'loose-belted lad'.

Plut.
Caes. 4 The senator Cicero was the first to see through Caesar's policies and to
fear them as one fears the smiling surface of the sea. He understood the
powerful character hidden beneath his kind and cheerful manner and said
that in almost everything he did Caesar was planning to become a tyrant. 15

In 63 B.C. there was an unsuccessful attempt at revolution led by a young
nobleman named Catiline. There were rumours that Caesar had been involved, but
the charge was never proved.

In the following year Caesar was praetor and in December Pompey returned
from the East. The war had lasted five years, Pompey had won some notable
victories and King Mithridates had committed suicide.

III.2 The Clodius scandal

Plut. Caes. 9 There were no political disturbances while Caesar was praetor, but his 62 B.C. domestic life was not quite so fortunate.

Publius Clodius came from a patrician family and was well-known as a wealthy man and an excellent speaker – but when it came to his scandalous and daring behaviour, there was no one in Rome to match him. 5

Clodius was in love with Pompeia, Caesar's wife, and she did nothing to discourage him. However, a close watch was kept on the women's apartments and Caesar's mother Aurelia was sensible enough to keep a close eye on his young wife. It was therefore difficult and dangerous for the two lovers to meet. 10

The Romans have a goddess whom they call Bona – the Good One. Men are not allowed to attend her sacred ceremonies, or even to be in the house when they are celebrated.

The festival is held at the house of a consul or praetor but, as the time approaches, they have to leave the house and take all the males with them. 15 The wife then takes over the house and gets it ready. The most important rites take place at night with much fun and games and lots of music.

Pompeia was in charge of this particular festival and Clodius thought he would be able to get in unnoticed because he had not yet started to grow a beard. So he dressed up as a young woman and went to the house disguised 20 as a musician. When he got there he found that the door was open and he got in without any trouble, helped by a slave-girl who was in on the secret.

Clodius was left for some time while the slave-girl ran off to tell Pompeia of his arrival. Eventually he became bored and began to wander about the large house. He did his best to keep away from the lamps but was found by 25 one of Aurelia's maids. She asked him to play with her, as one woman would with another. When Clodius refused she dragged him forward and asked him who he was and where he came from. Clodius said that he was waiting for Alba (this was the name of Pompeia's slave-girl) but his voice gave him away. Aurelia's maid immediately screamed and leapt away from 30 him into the light, shouting to the rest of the crowd that she had caught a man.

The women were panic-stricken. Aurelia stopped the ceremony and had everything covered up. Then she ordered the doors to be closed and went through the house with torches looking for Clodius. He was found where 35 he hid himself – in the room of the girl who had helped him get into the house. When the women realised who he was they threw him out of doors and immediately went off to tell their husbands what had happened, even though it was still the middle of the night.

On the next day word soon got round the city that Clodius had 40 committed sacrilege. People began to say that justice should be done, not only for the sake of those he had offended, but also for the sake of the city and the gods.

One of the tribunes drew up a charge of sacrilege against him. The most

powerful senators joined together and gave witness that he had committed   45
many dreadful crimes – not least of which was that of adultery with his
sister, the wife of Lucullus. They were eager to have Clodius condemned,
but the people came to his defence and terrified the jurors, who were afraid
of the mob.

Caesar immediately divorced Pompeia; but when he was called as a   50
witness in the trial, he said he knew nothing about the things with which
Clodius had been charged. It was a strange statement and the prosecutor
said to him, 'Why, then, did you divorce your wife?'. 'Because', said
Caesar, 'my wife should not even be under suspicion.' Some say that
Caesar's testimony was honest; others say that he just wanted to keep in   55
with the people, who were determined to save Clodius. At any rate,
Clodius was acquitted of the charge.

III.3 The return of Pompey

Plut. *Pomp.* 42 When he had sorted out all his arrangements in the East, Pompey set off
home with great pomp and ceremony. He stopped at Mytilene where he
watched the traditional poetry festival. All the poems had the same theme –
the deeds of Pompey. He was very pleased with the theatre in that city and
had sketches and plans of it drawn for him, as he had decided to build one   5
like it in Rome, only bigger and better.

Pompey hoped to return to Italy with more fame and glory than any man
before and he hoped that his family would be longing to see him again as
much as he was longing to see them; but there is a god whose job it is to
mix a dose of evil into every share of happiness given by Fortuna, and this   10
god had been working secretly for a long time to make Pompey's
homecoming a bitter one – for while he was away his wife Mucia had been
unfaithful. When Pompey was sure that this charge was true, he sent ahead
a letter to release her from their marriage.

As he came closer to Rome all sorts of rumours went ahead of him. Men   15
said that he would march into the city with his army and make himself
king. This caused a great commotion, so as soon as he set foot in Italy,   62 B.C.
Pompey calmed the situation by calling his troops together and speaking to
them. He thanked them warmly for all they had done for him; then he
ordered them to break up and go off to all the different cities where they   20
lived – but to be sure that they all met together outside Rome to celebrate
his triumph.

When word got around that the army had been disbanded, an amazing
thing happened. For when people saw Pompey the Great travelling along
with no weapons or armour and only a handful of friends just as though he   25
was coming home from his holidays, they came pouring out of the cities to
cheer him and they escorted him all the way to Rome. In fact he now had
more supporters behind him than he had in his army. If he had wanted to
destroy the Republic, he would not have needed his soldiers.

It was against the law for a general to enter the city before his triumph,   30

23

but it was the time of the elections and Pompey sent a message to the senate asking for the elections to be postponed so that he would be able to support a candidate in person. His request was opposed by the senator Cato and Pompey was refused permission.

However, Pompey admired Cato because he was outspoken and the only man to show any real concern about law and order. He was therefore keen to win Cato over in one way or another. Now Cato happened to have two nieces, and Pompey wanted to marry one himself and arrange for his son to marry the other. But Cato saw through Pompey's plan; he thought it was a form of corruption and did not want to be bribed by marriage alliances. In the meantime, Pompey was spending huge sums of money to get his friend Afranius elected consul. People actually used to go down to Pompey's gardens and collect their money. There was a lot of talk about this and Pompey was severely criticised.

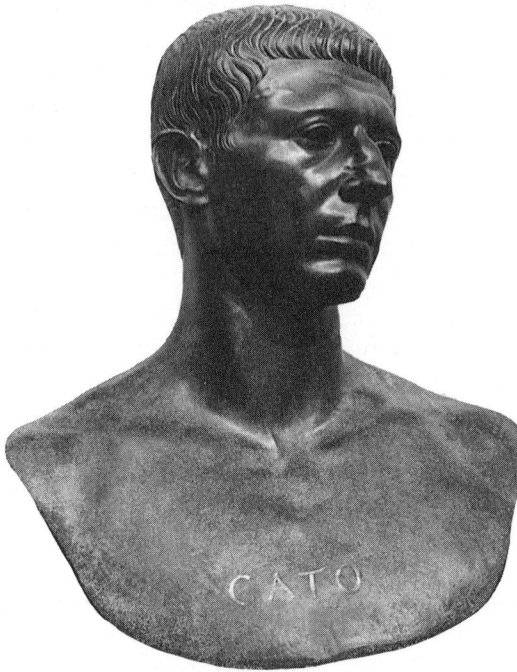

Triumph

61 B.C.

Plut.
Pomp. 45

So great was Pompey's triumph that even though the procession lasted two days there was not enough time for it all and many of the things which had been got ready for the display had to be left out. In fact there was enough left over for another triumph.

A triumphal procession. On the left can be seen a wooden litter with a trophy and two barbarian prisoners in chains.

At the front of the procession went men carrying placards showing the nations Pompey had conquered: Pontus, Armenia, Cappadocia, Paphlagonia, Media, Colchis, Spain, Albania, Syria, Cilicia, Mesopotamia, Phoenicia and Palestine, Judaea, Arabia. There were the pirates too whose power he had destroyed on sea and land. According to the placards he had captured 1,000 pirate strongholds, 900 of their cities and 800 of their ships, and he had founded 39 new cities for them to settle in.

Some of the placards told how Rome had once gathered 50 million drachmas in taxes but now, thanks to the new lands which Pompey had brought under Roman rule, she gathered 85 million drachmas. Furthermore Pompey was bringing into the public treasury coins, plates, goblets and urns of gold and silver worth 20,000 talents – apart from the money which he had shared out amongst each of his soldiers. The smallest of these shares was 1,500 drachmas!

There were many captives in the triumph – kings and queens of many lands with their children. There were huge numbers of trophies – one of each battle which Pompey or his officers had won.

But the most glorious thing for Pompey – the thing which no Roman had ever done before – was this: his first triumph had been over Africa, his second over Europe and now his last was over Asia, so that he seemed to have led the whole world prisoner through the streets of Rome.

Greek and Roman money

Greek	Roman
1 talent = 60 minae	1 aureus = 25 denarii
1 mina = 100 drachmae	1 denarius = 2 sestertii

1 drachma = 1 denarius

At this period, a legionary soldier earned 450 sestertii per annum, though Caesar later doubled this.

The pictures show two sides of the same gold coin – a Roman aureus of 71 B.C. celebrating Pompey's African triumph. The head wearing an elephant skin is a symbolic representation of Africa.

III.4 Problems with money

After his year as praetor, Caesar was appointed governor of Spain. He was due to leave Rome shortly after Pompey's triumph.

Plut.
Caes. 11 Caesar owed a lot of money and was finding it hard to arrange things with his creditors. They were making a lot of fuss and trying to prevent his leaving. He therefore had to ask the help of Crassus, the richest Roman of   5
them all. Crassus was an opponent of Pompey and needed a strong, fiery character like Caesar to help him. It was only after Crassus had guaranteed the sum of 830 talents that Caesar could go out to his province.

As he was crossing the Alps he came to a barbarian village which had only a handful of miserable inhabitants. Caesar's travelling companions   10
began to laugh at them and make jokes, and one of them said,

'Do you think that even here these fellows want to be magistrates, squabble for high positions and are all jealous of each other's rank?' Caesar answered in a serious voice, 'I would rather be the first man in this village than the second man in Rome.'   15

Plut.
Caes. 12 In Spain he marched as far as the outer sea, conquering all those tribes   61 B.C.
who would not obey Rome. He was just as successful when it came to arranging peace as he had been in finishing off the war. He established friendly relations between cities and was especially good at healing the disagreements between debtors and creditors.   20

When he finally left the province to return to Rome he had made a great name for himself; he had become rich and made his soldiers rich and they had saluted him as 'imperator'.[1] He intended to ask the senate for a triumph.

[1] A title of honour given to a victorious general by his soldiers.

III.5 A dilemma   60 B.C.

Plut.
Caes. 13 Caesar now found himself in a dilemma, for he arrived home just when the elections were being held for the consulship. The problem was that if a general wanted to hold a triumph he had to wait *outside* the city walls while the senate discussed his request whereas if he wanted to be a candidate for the consulship he had to be present *inside* the city. Caesar wrote to the   5
senate and asked permission to stand in the elections without entering the city. He said that his friends would represent him.

Many senators were ready to support this request, but Cato insisted that the law should be obeyed and he talked for so long about it that there was no time that day for a vote.   10

Caesar decided to give up his triumph and to enter for the elections instead.

III.6　The three-headed monster

Caesar was annoyed that he was not allowed to celebrate a triumph. He now discovered that Pompey was also in dispute with the senate.

Appian
Civil Wars
2.2.9
The war against Mithridates had increased Pompey's reputation and made him very powerful. At the end of the war he had made promises to various kings, rulers and cities and now asked the senate to confirm officially what he had done. Most of the senators, however, were jealous of Pompey and refused to do so. The strongest opposition to him came from Lucullus, the man who held the command against Mithridates before Pompey. Lucullus reckoned that the victory over Mithridates was his and not Pompey's, because he had left the king in such a weak state. Crassus took Lucullus' side over this.

Pompey was extremely angry and made friends with Caesar, promising under oath to support him for the consulship. Caesar immediately got Crassus to make friends with Pompey, and the three of them used their great influence to support each other's interests. The author Varro wrote about this coalition in a book which he called *The three-headed monster*.

This alliance was a private arrangement at first and it came as a surprise to most leading Romans. This is how Plutarch describes these events.

Plut.
Crassus 14
Caesar realised that without the help of Pompey and Crassus he had little hope for the future. He did not want to make one of them his enemy by making the other his friend, so he set about persuading them to make friends with each other. He kept pointing out to them that while they were busy attacking each other they were giving power to people like Cato and Cicero who would be nobodies if the two of them would only agree and rule Rome with their united power. They listened to Caesar and did make friends, and Caesar won the support of them both. In this way he gained a power which no one could stop and which he used to destroy the senate and the people. You see, he did not make Pompey greater by making him support Crassus, or Crassus greater by making him support Pompey – he made himself greater than anyone, by using them both!

Plut.
Caes. 14
Caesar now had Pompey and Crassus as a sort of bodyguard and he entered the elections for the consulship.

Caesar was elected overwhelmingly. However, his partner in the consulship was a man called Bibulus, who detested Caesar and had powerful friends in the senate.

Plut.
Caes. 14
As soon as Caesar was elected he proposed laws which were more like the laws of an extreme tribune than a consul – for to please the common people he brought forward all sorts of ideas for sharing out plots of land. In the senate the better sort of people opposed him. This gave him an excuse. He shouted and swore that the senate were high-handed and stubborn and it was their fault that he now had to go straight to the people with his ideas. So, with Crassus on the one side and Pompey on the other, he hurried off to a meeting of the people.

5

10

15

20

25

30

59
B.C.

35

40

Plut.
Pomp. 48 Pompey filled the city with his soldiers and controlled everything by
force. The crowd set upon Bibulus as he went down to the Forum with
Lucullus and Cato. They smashed to pieces the fasces carried by his lictors,   45
and someone tipped a bucket of dung over his head. The tribunes and
some others also received wounds and blows.

This was how Pompey and Caesar cleared their opponents from the
Forum so that they were able to pass the laws about the sharing out of land.
The people swallowed this bait and from now on they were prepared to eat   50
out of Caesar's hand and would vote for anything he wanted without
causing trouble.

More marriages

Plut.
Caes. 14 Caesar was trying to make more use of Pompey's influence. He therefore
arranged to engage his daughter Julia to him. She was already engaged to
Servilius Caepio, but Caesar said he would arrange for Servilius to marry   55
Pompey's daughter – though she too was already engaged, having been
promised to Sulla's son Faustus!

Shortly after this Caesar married Calpurnia and arranged that her father
Piso should be consul in the next year. Cato made a strong protest about all
this. 'This is intolerable!' he exclaimed. 'The government of this country is   60
being cheapened by all these marriage arrangements. To think that these
men can push each other forward for high positions and for commands of
provinces and armies by means of women!'

III.7   An unconquerable force

Suet.
Caes. 22 Caesar now had the goodwill of his father-in-law Piso, and his son-in-law
Pompey. He looked at all the available provinces and decided that Gaul was
the most likely to give him wealth and triumphs. At first he was just given
Cisalpine Gaul and Illyricum; this was the proposal of the tribune Vatinius.

Then the senate decided to add Transalpine Gaul as well. They were afraid that if it was denied to him, the common people would insist that he had it anyway. 5

Plutarch says that in going out to these provinces, Caesar seemed to take on a new lease of life. 58 B.C.

Plut.
Pomp. 51

The wars in Gaul raised Caesar up and made him great. He seemed to be far away from Rome and busy fighting, but all the time he was secretly and cunningly at work in the heart of Rome undermining Pompey. He was learning to control his army as though it was his own body. He was giving his soldiers a thorough training – and it was not to fight barbarians. In fact he used his battles against them to keep his own men fit, as though he had sent them out for a day's hunting! He was making his army unconquerable and terrifying. 10 15

Caesar and his army

Plut.
Caes. 16

Caesar's men were so enthusiastic and ready to serve him that men who were quite ordinary when fighting for other generals became irresistible and unconquerable when fighting for Caesar. Here are some examples:

In a sea-battle off Marseilles, a soldier called Acilius clambered aboard an enemy ship. His right hand was lopped off with a sword but he kept tight hold of his shield with his left and smashed it into the faces of the enemy. He scattered them all and so captured the ship. 5

Once, in Britain, the centurions leading the column stumbled into a river swamp and the enemy suddenly attacked them. Before Caesar's eyes an ordinary soldier dived into the middle of the fighting and laid about him with great courage until the barbarians turned and ran and the centurions were saved. Then last of all, he plunged into the muddy stream and with 10

Relief carving from the time of Caesar and Pompey. One of the few contemporary pictures of military uniform. Some people think the relief shows a soldier joining the army; others think it shows a young man being enrolled as a citizen.

great difficulty, half swimming, half wading, he came back to dry land. Caesar and his men were astounded and came to meet him shouting with delight. But the soldier was absolutely miserable. Bursting into tears he threw himself at Caesar's feet begging pardon for losing his shield! 15

Plut. Caes. 17 Caesar made his men eager to do such glorious deeds in two ways. First, he was very generous in handing out rewards and so his soldiers realised that he was not making a fortune out of the wars to spend on himself and have a life of luxury and ease. Instead he was saving it up to reward brave actions 20 and he was getting no more of it for himself than he was giving to the soldiers who earned it. Second, he showed that he was ready to face any danger himself and he never dodged the hardest jobs.

Suet. Caes. 65 He was not interested in how rich a soldier was or whether he had a good character – so long as he had courage. He treated them all with equal 25 discipline and kindness, but when the enemy were nearby he was extremely strict. He would never tell his men when they were going to march out to battle but kept them on the alert and ready to follow him out at a moment's notice wherever he wanted to go. He often did this when there was no need, especially in the rain or on a holiday. He would sneak 30 out of the camp, day or night, and lead them off. On these occasions he always made sure that he led them a good long march to sort out the stragglers.

Suet. Caes. 67 When he spoke to his army he did not call them 'soldiers' but 'comrades' which is much more flattering. He kept them very smart, equipping them 35 with weapons inlaid with silver and gold. This was partly for show but also so that in battle the men would keep tight hold of them for fear of losing them!

III.8 Uneasy years

Meanwhile in Rome, the year 57 B.C. saw Pompey given five years' command of the corn supply. 'Under his charge', writes Plutarch, 'were placed all the harbours, markets and food supplies – in fact everything related to navigation and agriculture.'

During 58 and 57 B.C. Caesar won three important victories and Plutarch tells us 5 that when the news reached Rome he was awarded a public thanksgiving which lasted a fortnight.

Some senators then began to say that Caesar should be recalled because Gaul was at peace. Caesar himself, however, thought that the job was incomplete and wanted his command to be extended. He also knew that Pompey's command in 10 charge of the corn supply would outlast his own by two years.

Plut. Pomp. 51 When Caesar crossed the Alps to spend the winter in the city of Luca, a 56 B.C. huge crowd of people, both men and women, flocked to greet him there. There were 200 senators in the crowd, including Pompey and Crassus. Caesar loaded them all up with money and promises and sent them away, 15 and he came to the following arrangement with Pompey and Crassus: the two of them were to stand for election as consuls and Caesar would help them by sending large numbers of his soldiers to Rome to vote for them. As soon as they were elected they were to make sure of provinces and armies for themselves and for Caesar to be given another five years of command in Gaul.

When news of this deal spread, the leading men of the senate were indignant. In protest, none of them would stand as candidates in the elections. However, Cato persuaded Domitius to stand with him by saying, 'We are not fighting these three tyrants just to decide who should be made consuls – we are fighting for Liberty.' But when Pompey's supporters saw the honest strength of Cato they were frightened that he would win the support of the whole senate and that the decent people of Rome would go over to him, so they sent a group of armed men to stop Domitius entering the Forum. They killed the torch-bearer who was leading Domitius and his friends and put the rest to flight. Cato was the last to retreat. He was wounded in the right arm while fighting to defend Domitius.

Plut.
Pomp. 52 In this way Pompey and Crassus obtained the offices they wanted. Then they introduced laws, with the help of one of the tribunes. Caesar, as had been agreed, had his command continued for another five years; Crassus was put in charge of Syria and the war against the Parthians; Pompey got the whole of Africa, both Spanish provinces and four legions, but he lent Caesar two of them for the war in Gaul.

Plut.
Pomp. 40 At the end of the year Pompey opened the beautiful and famous theatre which he built for the Romans. Close beside it he built himself a new house – it was like a rowing boat bobbing along behind a great ship. Up till then he had lived in a modest and simple house. The new one was rather more splendid but it was certainly not big enough to make people jealous. The man who owned it after Pompey was amazed when he first went in to see how small it was and wanted to know where on earth Pompey the Great went to eat his dinner.

Part of a model of ancient Rome with Pompey's theatre in the foreground.

31

The theatre of Pompey

Many senators considered the theatre a very low form of entertainment. So for many years Rome only had temporary theatres made of wood. Pompey's theatre was the first to be made of stone.

It was part of a huge complex. At the top of the seats was a temple to Victorious Venus and behind the stage was a portico with rooms for storing equipment. People could meet here if it was raining. There were also gardens, fountains and shady walks, where works of art were put on display.

To celebrate the opening of his theatre Pompey put on competitions in athletics and music in honour of the Gods. There were wild beast fights too in which 500 lions were killed, but the most terrifying event of all was a battle of elephants.

The writer Velleius considered that Pompey's career had reached its highest point at this time.

5

10

At the beginning of the third century A.D. the emperor Septimius Severus set up a huge plan of Rome in marble. Fragments of this plan are still found from time to time. This is one of the best preserved and shows the theatre of Pompey.

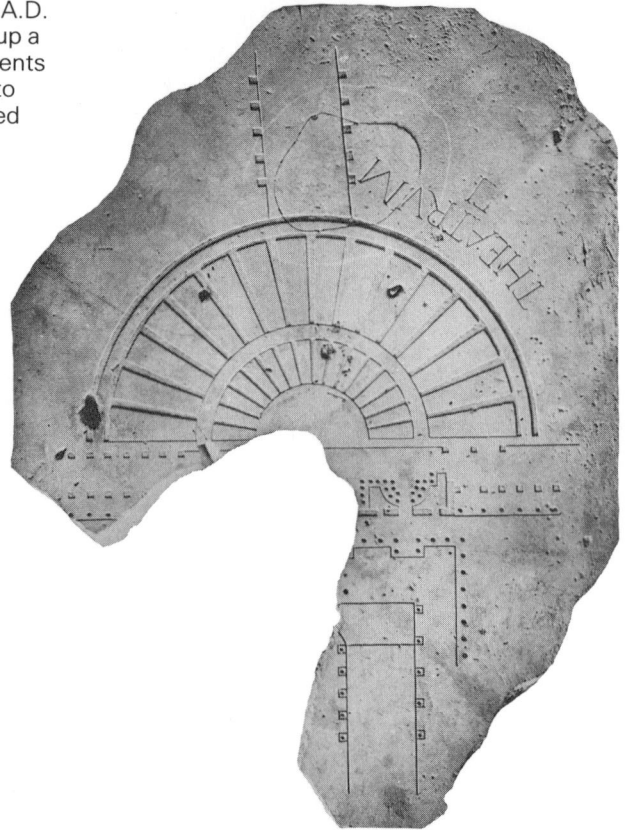

An aerial photograph of the area called 'The Field of Mars' in Pompey's day.

III.9 Pompey and his wife

Plut.
Pomp. 53 All this won Pompey many admirers and supporters. On the other hand, many people were annoyed with him for, instead of going out to his provinces, he handed them and his armies over to his friends while he spent his time going with his wife, Julia, from one Italian pleasure resort to the other. This was either because he loved her or because she loved him so much that he did not have the heart to leave her. In fact there was a lot of ill-natured gossip about the young girl's love for her husband – after all, Pompey was old enough to be her father. However, he was always faithful to his wife. His manners were dignified but always friendly and gentle, and women found this most attractive. 5

10

Once, when the elections were being held to choose the aediles, a fight broke out. Many people near Pompey were killed and he was spattered all over with blood. He changed his clothes and his slaves went running home with them shouting loudly. When his young wife, who was pregnant, saw his blood-stained toga she fainted and they had great difficulty bringing her round. 15

Because of the shock she had a miscarriage. After this even the people who disapproved of Pompey's friendship with Caesar could not blame him for loving his wife as he did.

She became pregnant again later and had a baby girl – but she died when the baby was born and the little girl only lived for a few days. 20 54 B.C.

Pompey made arrangements to bury her near his villa at Alba, but the people seized the body by force and carried it to the Field of Mars to be buried. They did this more in pity for the young wife, than in honour of Caesar and Pompey. 25

III.10 A stormy sea and a dangerous disease

Plut.
Pomp. 53 After the death of Julia the city surged up like a stormy sea and angry speeches divided the people. The marriage alliance was now at an end, and though it may have concealed the two men's love of power it had done nothing to diminish it.

After a short time the news also came that Crassus had died in Parthia – 53 B.C. so another obstacle to civil war had been removed. Through fear of him, Caesar and Pompey had somehow or other managed to treat each other fairly.

That year the system of government nearly broke down.

Plut.
Caes. 28 Candidates in the elections actually set up pay tables in public and shamelessly paid out bribes to the crowd. The people took the money and went along to the Forum not so much to vote for the man who had hired them as to fight for him with bows and arrows, swords and slings. Often they would pollute the rostra with blood and corpses before they broke up 10

and left the city tossing about like a ship without a helmsman. 15

Soon many people dared to say openly that the only cure for the disease of the state was monarchy, and that this cure should be used since it was offered by the gentlest of surgeons – by which they meant Pompey.

Plut.
Pomp. 54 Bibulus, who was an enemy of Pompey, proposed in the senate that Pompey should be made sole consul. In this way the city would either be 20 saved from the rioting or it would become the slave of the strongest man. This seemed a strange proposal, considering the man who made it, and when Cato rose to his feet he gave the impression that he was going to speak against it. When silence fell, he spoke as follows:

'I myself would not have introduced the measure which now lies before 25 us. But now that someone else has introduced it, I would urge you to give it your support. Any government is better than no government, and who can govern better than Pompey in these difficult times?'

The senate agreed to the proposal and Pompey was elected sole consul 52 B.C. for the year. 30

Cornelia

Plut.
Pomp. 55 Pompey now married Cornelia, the daughter of Metellus Scipio. She had been married before but had recently been left a widow. (Her first husband Publius, the son of Crassus, had died in Parthia.) This young woman had many charming qualities apart from her youth and beauty. She was well read, played the lyre and studied geometry; she also used to go to lectures 35 on philosophy and was a very attentive listener. Yet she was not at all tiresome or pretentious like most intellectual girls. No one could find fault with her father's family and reputation, but some people disapproved of the marriage because she was so much younger than Pompey. They said that her age made her more suitable for one of his sons. 40

Order restored

After some difficulty, Pompey managed to bring order to Rome and he chose his father-in-law, Metellus Scipio, to share the consulship for the last five months. The senate voted that Pompey should be allowed to keep his provinces for another four years and that he should be given 1,000 talents each year to feed and pay his soldiers. 45

III.11   Caesar the conqueror

While these events were taking place at Rome, Caesar was fighting wars in Gaul.

Plut.
Caes. 15 It was in these wars that Caesar proved that he was the greatest of all generals even when compared with Pompey himself whose fame at that time was in full bloom and reaching up to the sky. For Caesar fought more battles and killed more of the enemy than any other general. Although the 5 war in Gaul lasted less than ten years he took over 800 cities by storm,

conquered 300 tribes and fought pitched battles at different times against three million men. One million of these he killed in hand-to-hand fighting and took many more prisoner.

The invasion of Britain

Plut.
Caes. 23
One of his most daring and glorious deeds was the invasion of Britain. For he was the first man to go out with a fleet upon the waters of the western Ocean and to sail through the Atlantic sea with an army to wage war. The island was said to be unbelievably big and caused great arguments amongst many writers. Some of them said that it did not even exist and never had! They said that accounts of it – even its name – were lies. 10

15

    In attempting to invade Britain Caesar was spreading the power of Rome beyond the boundaries of the known world. Twice he crossed to the island from the coast of Gaul and fought many battles. He did more harm to the enemy than good to his own men, however, for the Britons lived in miserable poverty and had nothing worth taking. He decided to withdraw his troops before the war was completely finished but he took hostages from the king and imposed tribute. Then he sailed away. 55-54 B.C.

20

The wars in Gaul

The siege of Alesia

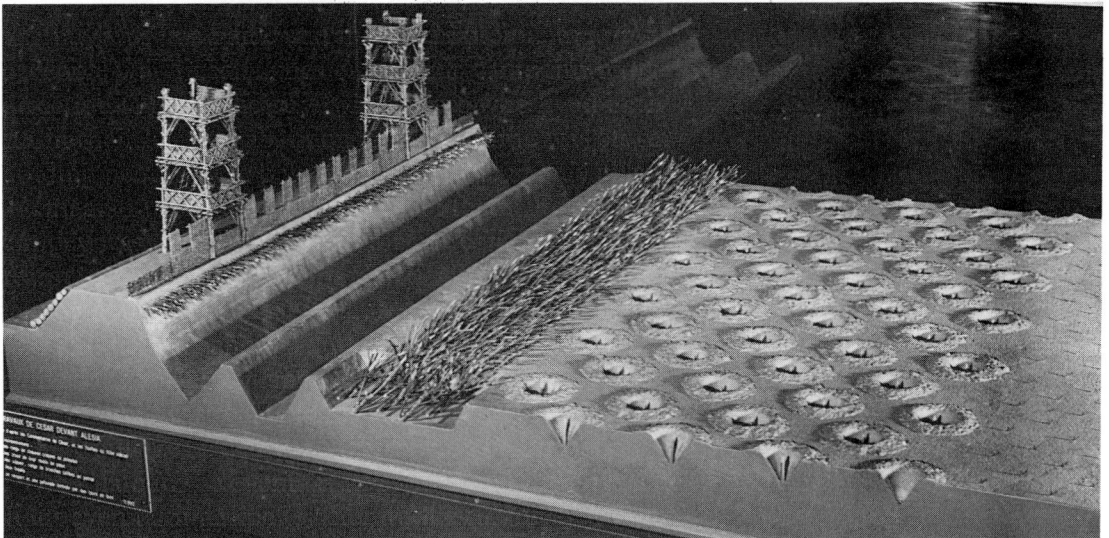

In 52 B.C. Caesar defeated a massive revolt of the Gauls led by Vercingetorix. This model shows part of the siege works which Caesar built around the town of Alesia, where Vercingetorix had taken refuge. The model is based on Caesar's own account and on excavations at the site. There were two rings of siege works. (This picture shows one.) The inner ring, nine miles (13km) long, was to prevent Vercingetorix escaping. The outer ring, thirteen miles (21km) long, was to prevent other forces coming to his rescue. Caesar's army, which was in the middle, beat off the attack of the relieving forces and Vercingetorix had to surrender. He was later executed when Caesar celebrated his triumph in Rome.

Alesia

Uxellodunum

NARBONESE
GAUL

ALPS

CISALPINE
GAUL

R. Rubicon

Ravenna

Marseilles

Luca

Ariminum

NEARER
SPAIN

Rome

Naples

FURTHER
SPAIN

M E D

Gades

I
T
E

Utica

SICILY

AFRICA

Thapsus

0 ————— 500 km

0 ————— 300 miles

The Roman World at the time of Caesar and Pompey

DACIA

BLACK SEA

PONTUS

ARMENIA

ILLYRICUM

Dyrrachium

Brindisium

Pharsalus

Actium

Corinth

Mytilene

Pergamum

PARTHIA

SYRIA

CILICIA
Taurus Mts

RHODES

CYPRUS

CRETE

MEDITERRANEAN SEA

JUDAEA

Alexandria

Pelusium

R. Nile

RED SEA

The siege of Uxellodunum

This siege took place in 51 B.C. and was one of the last major actions of the Gallic wars. The account which follows was written in 44 B.C. by one of Caesar's generals. It is part of the book he wrote to complete Caesar's own account of the war.

Uxellodunum was in south-western Gaul, in the area now called the Dordogne. A food convoy had been captured by Caesar's commander on the spot, but the townsfolk were still holding out and Caesar decided to go there himself.

Caes.
Gallic Wars
8.40-44

Caesar's arrival at Uxellodunum was completely unexpected. He saw that the town was surrounded by siege works and that the enemy had no chance of escaping if the town was attacked. He also discovered from deserters that the people in the town had a good supply of food; so he began to try to cut off the enemy from their water.

The town of Uxellodunum was built on a hill. There was a sheer drop all the way round and at the bottom was a river which ran through the valley and nearly surrounded the town.

Caesar cut off the townsfolk from the river, so there was just one point left for them to draw water. This was just below the town wall, where a great spring of water gushes out. (It is on this side of the town that the circuit of the river is broken for about 300 feet (90 metres).) All the Romans hoped and prayed that the townsfolk could be cut off from this water, but Caesar alone saw how it could be done.

He began by moving mantlets up to the hill and started to construct a ramp. It was hard work and there was continual fighting, for the townsfolk came running down from above and hurled their missiles from a safe distance. Our men were determined to make their way up the hill and this caused many casualties. But in spite of this they pushed the mantlets forward and worked with every effort to overcome the difficulties of the area. At the same time they dug mines towards the head of the spring. This was not a dangerous job and could be done without arousing the suspicions of the enemy.

The ramp was built up to a height of 60 feet (18 metres) and on top of it was placed a turret 10 storeys high. It did not, of course, reach the level of the walls because that would have been impossible, but it did look down over the top of the spring. Artillery was placed on top of the turret and missiles were hurled down onto the approach to the spring.

It was now very dangerous for the townsfolk to get water. As a result, not only the cattle and pack-animals but also a large number of the enemy themselves began to suffer desperately from thirst. Terrified by this calamity, they filled tubs with grease, pitch and pieces of lath, set fire to them, and rolled them down on our siege works. At the same time they made a fierce charge so that the fighting would be too dangerous for the Romans to try to put out the fire.

Suddenly a great flame shot up in the middle of our siege works. In fact, anything that was thrown over the cliff edge rolled straight onto the ramp and mantlets, and set fire to whatever got in the way. On the other hand,

5

10

15

20

25

30

35

40

45

our soldiers faced everything in the bravest of spirits. The fight was dangerous and their position was inferior, but they were fighting in a high place and could be seen by the rest of the army. There was a lot of cheering from both groups and every man wanted to be as conspicuous as possible. They all faced up to the weapons and flames of the enemy, and hoped that 50 their bravery would be noticed and commended by their colleagues.

When Caesar saw that many of his men had been wounded, he ordered some cohorts to climb up the hill on every side of the town and shout as if they had taken possession of the walls. This action terrified the townsfolk. Since they did not know what was happening in the rest of the town they 55 recalled the men from the attack on the siege works and placed them around the walls. As soon as the fighting stopped, our men put out the flames or cut out any parts of our siege works that were still alight.

The townsfolk were still determined to resist and refused to give in, even though they had lost large numbers through thirst. But in the end the 60 streams which fed the spring were cut off and diverted by the mines. The everlasting spring dried up and the townsfolk became so desperate that they thought it must be the will of the gods, not the work of man. There was no choice left for them; they had to surrender.

Caesar knew that his leniency was well known and had no fears that 65 people would think he had a cruel nature if he now acted more harshly than usual. He could see no success for his plans if more of the enemy came up with similar ideas in other areas, so he decided on a punishment which would set an example and deter others. He therefore cut off the hands of all those who had carried arms, while sparing their lives. In this way he made 70 it clear to all what the punishment was for wrongdoers.

III.12   A dispute

Plut.
Pomp. 56

So when Caesar's friends heard of the privileges which the senate had granted Pompey for bringing peace to the city, they wanted to know why Caesar should not be given the same. After all he was fighting war after war on behalf of Rome. They said that he deserved either to be made consul again or to be allowed to remain in command of his armies in Gaul for a 5 further period of time; otherwise somebody else would be sent to take over from him and so rob him of the glory. Pompey said that Caesar should be allowed to stand for the consulship even though he was absent from Rome, but Cato and the other senators objected. They said that Caesar should put down his weapons and become an ordinary citizen again before he started 10 asking his fellow citizens for favours! Pompey did not argue with this and people began to wonder what his feelings towards Caesar really were. He also sent a message to Caesar asking him to return the two legions which he had lent him earlier. Caesar saw the real reason behind the request, but still sent the soldiers back. First, however, he gave them each a present of 250 15 drachmas.

Plut.
Pomp. 51
Caes. 29
What is more he kept sending back to Rome enormous amounts of gold and silver, and all sorts of rich booty which he won in his endless wars. All this was for bribes. It was to help aediles, praetors, consuls – and their wives – with their expenses. The tribune Curio accepted money to pay his endless debts and the consul Aemilius Paulus took 1,500 talents which he used to build his famous and beautiful basilica in the Forum. 20

It was said that a centurion who had been sent to Rome by Caesar was standing outside the place where the senate was meeting when word came out that they would not give Caesar a longer time to govern his provinces. 25 The centurion tapped his hand on his sword hilt and said, 'They won't, but this will!'

III. 13   A stamp of the foot

Plut.
Pomp. 57
At this time Pompey fell dangerously sick in Naples. When he recovered, the people of the city offered up sacrifices in thanksgiving and the people of the neighbouring cities did the same. The rejoicing spread, and soon every city in Italy, large and small, was holding celebrations which lasted many days. As Pompey travelled back to Rome no place he passed through was 5 big enough to hold all the people who came flooding in from every direction to cheer him on. The roads and villages and harbours were crowded with people sacrificing and feasting. Crowds of people with garlands in their hair and flaming torches in their hands greeted him and ran beside him pelting him with flowers. It was all a sight of glittering 10 beauty – yet men say it was the main cause of the war which followed, for all this rejoicing went to Pompey's head and he became over-confident. He began to sneer at Caesar's power, and he decided that it was a waste of time and effort to raise and organise an army – after all it would be easier to knock Caesar down than it had been to raise him up. When people said, 'If 15 Caesar does march on Rome we don't see any troops ready to resist him', Pompey smiled calmly and answered, 'Don't worry; I have only to stamp my foot on the ground in any part of Italy and whole armies of infantry and cavalry will spring up!'

III. 14   The crisis draws near

Plut.
Caes. 30-31
Antony 5
Caesar now wrote a letter in which he said that if he laid down his arms   50 B.C. Pompey should do the same. The tribune Curio read this letter to the people on behalf of Caesar and the people cheered and clapped; in fact some of them actually hung Curio with garlands of flowers as though he was a victorious athlete. Antony, who was another tribune, had received a 5 similar letter from Caesar and read it out loud to the people, even though the consuls tried to stop him. But in the senate Pompey's father-in-law Scipio proposed that if Caesar did not give up his command by a certain day then he would be declared a public enemy.

Soon more letters arrived from Caesar, and Cicero began to hope that he could arrange a compromise. The consul Lentulus, however, would have none of this. 10

Plut.
Caes. 31 Instead he began to hurl insults at Curio and Mark Antony and he actually bundled them out of the senate house. The two tribunes immediately hired waggons and left the city disguised as slaves. They hurried to tell Caesar what had happened. As soon as they saw him they shouted angrily that 15 Rome was in chaos and not even the tribunes of the people had freedom of speech. They said that anyone who spoke up for justice was persecuted and in danger of his life.

Plut.
Caes. 31 So it was that Caesar was given his excuse to take action, and was able to arouse his soldiers by pointing at these men of high importance who had 20 been driven from Rome in fear.

Suet.
Caes. 30 This was his excuse for civil war, but he is believed to have had other reasons. Pompey used to say that he wanted to throw everything into confusion because he could not afford to complete the works he had begun; people had high expectations about his return and he could not live up to 25 them. Others say that he was afraid of having to give an account of his first consulship because he had acted against the laws, omens and vetoes.

III. 15   The crossing of the Rubicon

Caesar was at the southern boundary of his province when the tribunes reached him. He knew that if he led his army across the border he would be committing treason. Most of his soldiers were on the other side of the Alps and he only had about 300 cavalry and 6,000 legionaries with him. He decided that instead of waiting for his army to join him he would move quickly and take his enemies at 5 Rome by surprise.

Extracts from Caesar's own account

Caes.
Civil War
1.5-8 The tribunes immediately left the city and went to join Caesar. At that time he was at Ravenna, waiting for a reply to his very lenient demands. He hoped that some sense of fairness might bring things to a peaceable conclusion. 10

On the following days the senate met outside the city. Pompey praised the courage and consistency of the senate, detailed the resources at his command, and told them that he had ten legions ready. He also claimed to have certain knowledge that Caesar was unpopular with the soldiers and could not persuade them to defend him or follow him. 15

The senate dealt with the remaining business at once. It was decided to raise troops and to make Pompey a grant from the treasury.

The levy of troops was held throughout Italy and weapons were requisitioned; money was demanded from the Italian towns and removed from the temples. All laws of men and gods were thrown into confusion. 20

Caesar then called his troops together and made a speech to them, in which he referred to the fate of the tribunes.

'A new precedent has been set in our state. The tribunes' right of veto has been removed by armed force. Sulla stripped the tribunes of every other form of power, but he did leave them their veto. Pompey did appear to have restored their powers, but now he has taken away the privileges they had before.'

Caesar went on to claim that the senate had never before declared a state of emergency in a situation like this. Finally he reminded the troops of their successes in Gaul and Germany.

All the soldiers present shouted that they were ready to take action against the wrongs done to their leader and the tribunes of the people. When Caesar saw that they were so willing, he set out for Ariminum with them. There he met the tribunes who had fled to him. He called the rest of the legions from their winter quarters and ordered them to follow after him. At that time he only had the thirteenth legion with him. He had summoned it at the beginning of the troubles and the others had not arrived yet.

Suetonius' account

Suet. Caes. 31-2 He sent some cohorts ahead secretly and then, to shake off any suspicion of what he was going to do, he went to a public show. Next he inspected plans of a new gladiatorial school which he was going to build and then he went, as he often did, to join a crowd of friends at a party.

But when the sun went down he borrowed some mules from a nearby bakery, harnessed them to his carriage and set out secretly with a few friends. Then his lamps blew out and he lost his way and wandered about for a long time until, as dawn was breaking, he met a man who gave him directions and he hurried on foot along narrow paths back to the main road.

When he caught up with his cohorts they had arrived at the river Rubicon. This little stream marked the boundary of Caesar's province. He paused on the bank as he thought what a step he was taking, then he turned to the men behind him. 'We can still turn back – it's not too late', he said, 'but once we cross that little bridge, it's war.'

As he stood there hesitating, the gods gave a sign. Not far off there appeared a gigantic figure – a man of wonderful beauty – playing upon a pipe of reeds. Shepherds came running down to listen to his music and many of the legionaries even left their ranks to listen. Amongst these soldiers were some buglers. The stranger snatched one of their bugles and went leaping down to the river. With a mighty blast he sounded the attack and waded towards the far bank. Then Caesar shouted, 'Let us go where we are led by the gods and our treacherous foes! The die is cast!'

And so he crossed the river with his army.

IV   The defeat of Pompey

IV.1   Panic and rumour

Plut.
Pomp. 60
Word that Caesar had crossed the Rubicon hurtled towards Rome and   49 B.C.
struck the city a blow of terror, causing such an uproar of panic as had
never been known before. Immediately the whole senate ran with the
magistrates at top speed to Pompey, but when Tullus asked him about the
army and the defence of the city, Pompey hesitated and said timidly, 'I   5
have ready the soldiers Caesar sent me and I think I can assemble an army
of 30,000 out of those who have been called up before.' When he heard this
Tullus cried out, 'Pompey, you have deceived us!' and he advised the
senate to send men to negotiate with Caesar. Then a man called Favonius
spoke up. He was a good man really, but he often said rude or awkward   10
things, thinking that he was imitating the straightforward way that Cato
spoke. 'Stamp your foot on the ground', he said, 'and make the armies
spring up as you promised.' Pompey took this ill-timed joke meekly.

Then the senator Cato advised that Pompey should be made
commander-in-chief with unlimited power, adding that it was a job of men   15
who caused great problems to solve them. Then he set out immediately for
Sicily which was his province by lot. The other senators who had provinces
did the same.

Almost the whole of Italy was in a panic and it was impossible to know
what was happening. People who lived in the countryside came tumbling   20
in haste from every direction to enter the city, while those who lived in the
city were tumbling out in their haste to abandon it – everything was stormy
and confused. Law-abiding people were powerless while the unruly classes
were so strong that the magistrates could hardly control them. Fear swept
over everyone and Pompey was given no time to think. People bombarded   25
him with their own fears, worries and problems. It was impossible for him
to get any real information about the enemy because people reported all
sorts of rumours to him and became annoyed if he would not believe them.
As a result he was having to change his plans twice a day! In the end, he
officially declared a state of civil war. He ordered all the senators to follow   30
him and declared that he would regard anyone who stayed behind as a
supporter of Caesar. Then, late in the evening, he abandoned the city. The
consuls fled too, without even taking time to offer up the sacrifices which
are usually made at the outbreak of war.

But even now, amongst all that fear and panic, Pompey was a man to be   35
envied. Everybody loved him – even those who found fault with him as a
general. Those who left the city for their freedom were far fewer than those
who left because they could not desert Pompey.

IV.2 Caesar in pursuit

Having crossed the Rubicon, Caesar occupied Picenum, Umbria and Etruria, and was joined by the Twelfth Legion which had marched with all speed from Gaul.

Plut.
Caes. 34-5

Then he marched against the town of Corfinium and camped nearby. Domitius, who was defending Corfinium with 30 cohorts, gave up hope and asked his doctor, who was a slave, for some poison. He took what he was given and drank it, intending to die. 5

Shortly afterwards Domitius got to hear that Caesar showed great clemency to his captives, and he began to have regrets about his foolish decision. Then his doctor cheered him up; he told him that it was not poison he had drunk but a sleeping potion. Domitius was overjoyed; he got 10 up, went off to find Caesar and shook him by the hand. Caesar let him go free – and he immediately deserted to Pompey again.

When the news of all this reached Rome, men became more cheerful and some of the fugitives turned back.

Meanwhile Caesar took over the troops of Domitius and marched against 15 Pompey himself.

A letter from Pompey

This letter survives in a collection of Cicero's private correspondence. It was written in 49 B.C. on February 20th. Pompey was in Canusium, a town about 100 miles north of Brundisium. This area of Italy is called Apulia.

Gnaeus Magnus sends his greetings to Cicero
I hope you are well. I was glad to read your letter. For in it I recognised 5 again the courage you have always shown in the interests of national safety. The consuls have joined my army in Apulia. In the name of your exceptional and unceasing patriotism, I strongly urge you to join me so that together we can plan how to help and rescue our sorely afflicted country. I think you should travel by the Appian Way and proceed quickly to 10 Brundisium.

Cicero, the leading public speaker of his day, had a distinguished and varied career. Many of his writings still survive.

The retreat of Pompey

Plut.
Pomp. 60

Pompey had by now entered the town of Brundisium where he found plenty of transport ships. He put the two consuls and thirty cohorts of soldiers aboard and sent them ahead to Dyrrachium. Now he barricaded the gates of Brundisium and posted his lightest-armed soldiers along the 20 walls. He ordered the people of the city to stay quietly inside their houses while he dug trenches everywhere in the city, and in the bottom of these trenches he fixed sharpened stakes. Only two streets were left open – the streets which led down to the sea. Without rushing he put the rest of his army aboard the transport ships and on the third day he gave a signal to the 25 men who were still guarding the walls. They made a dash for the sea and hurried aboard the ships, which carried them over to Dyrrachium.

When Caesar noticed that there was no one guarding the wall, he realised that Pompey was escaping and he hurried to catch him. His troops would have stumbled into the trenches and fallen on the stakes if the people of Brundisium had not warned him. Instead he circled the city only to find that by now all Pompey's transport ships were out at sea – except for two which had only a few soldiers aboard.

Pompey's supporters

Plut.
Pomp. 64
Pompey had now gathered together a large force. His navy was quite irresistible. He had 500 heavy war ships and countless light galleys and battle cruisers. He had 7,000 cavalry – all the best young men of Rome were in it, young men of ancient families, of wealth and courage. His infantry was a mixture of good and bad and needed training. At their training sessions he did not just sit by and watch, but joined in as if he were still in his prime. The men were greatly encouraged to see Pompey the Great, who was only two years short of sixty, competing with the best of them in the full armour of a foot soldier, or else training with the cavalry – drawing his sword easily while his horse was at full gallop and putting it back just as easily into its scabbard. In javelin practice he was not only accurate – he could throw his weapon further than many of the young men.

Each day kings of nations and princes kept coming to join him and there were enough of the leading men of Rome in his camp for him to hold a full meeting of the senate.

Amongst the others Cicero the great orator came to join him and also a man called Tidius Sextius who was extremely old and lame in one leg. When he arrived everybody laughed and jeered at him, but when Pompey saw him he stood up and ran forward to meet him – for he thought it was a great compliment that a man so old and helpless should prefer danger with Pompey to safety at home.

And Brutus came. This man's father had been executed by Pompey in Gaul. He was a man of high principles and until now he had never spoken a word to Pompey, and pretended not to know him when they met, for he considered Pompey to be his father's murderer. But now he believed that
Plut.
Brutus 4
Pompey was defending Liberty and he thought it was his duty to put the good of Rome first before his own feelings, and so he came to Pompey's camp. We are told that Pompey was so delighted to see him and admired him so much for what he had done that he rose from his seat when Brutus came and in front of everybody hugged him and said that he was a better man than himself.

A meeting of the senate was held in Pompey's camp. At Cato's suggestion, it was decreed that no Roman should be killed – except on the battlefield – and that no Roman city should be plundered. This made people support Pompey even more strongly, for they thought that anyone who did not now want Pompey to win was an enemy of gods and men.

Caesar heads for Rome

Plut.
Caes. 35

Caesar wanted to follow Pompey at once, but he was short of ships so he
turned back in the direction of Rome. He had become master of the whole
of Italy in sixty days, and no blood had been shed.

70

Plut.
Pomp. 62

A few days later he entered Rome and took possession of it. He treated
everyone with kindness and calmed their fears. The only exception was
Metellus, a tribune who tried to stop Caesar taking money from the
treasury. Caesar threatened to kill him and added 'It's much more difficult
for me to say that than to do it.'

75

The Temple of Saturn

Macrobius
Saturnalia
1.8

The Roman people chose the Temple of Saturn for their treasury either
because no theft was ever committed when Saturn lived in Italy or because
private property did not exist under his rule.

The poet Lucan (39–65 A.D.) describes Caesar's visit to the treasury:

Lucan
Civil War
III. 153-9, 161-8

Metellus was removed and at once the temple was thrown open.
Then the Tarpeian Rock re-echoed, witnessing with loud grating that the
doors were flung back. Then came forth from the temple the treasure of the
Roman People, untouched for many a year: spoils from the wars with
Hannibal and Perseus, the booty from defeated Philip and everything
which Pyrrhus left to you, Rome, in his fearful flight; everything which our
thrifty ancestors had gathered, all the tribute sent from the wealthy peoples

5

10

The Temple of Saturn.

of Asia, and everything that the Crete of King Minos gave to Metellus the conqueror; all that Cato brought back across the seas from distant Cyprus. Finally came the wealth of the East, the treasure of captive kings brought from afar and carried by in Pompey's triumph. Then for the first time was Rome poorer than a Caesar. 15

IV.3 The fighting begins

Plut.
Caes. 36
Pomp. 65
Next he led an army into Spain where he again showed that he could be a merciful conqueror. Having captured and defeated Pompey's supporters, he let the commanders go free and took the soldiers into his own army. Then he crossed back over the Alps and marched quickly through Italy. He crossed the sea from Brundisium and landed in Greece. 5

Caesar had a prisoner of war who was a friend of Pompey. His name was Vibullius and Caesar sent him to Pompey with the proposal that they should hold a conference, disband their armies within three days, swear an oath of friendship and return to Italy. Pompey thought this was another trap. He marched quickly down to the shore and seized possession of every 10
point which would be a useful landing-place for an army or anyone else coming in from the sea.

The result was that every wind which blew brought Pompey grain or soldiers or money, while Caesar was short of supplies both on land and sea.

IV.4   Dyrrachium

Plut.
Caes. 39
Mark Antony now managed to sail in from Brundisium with extra forces and Caesar felt confident enough to challenge Pompey to fight. Caesar was desperately short of supplies, but his soldiers dug up a root of some sort, mixed it with milk and ate it. Once, they baked it and made some loaves. They then ran up to the enemy fortifications and threw some of them over 5
the walls. They tossed the loaves from one to another, shouting that as long as the earth gave roots such as these they would not stop besieging Pompey. Pompey would not allow these loaves to be shown or the words to be reported to the rest of the army, for his soldiers were disheartened and frightened by the savage toughness of the enemy, who seemed to them like 10
wild animals.

There were now a lot of skirmishes round Pompey's fortifications at Dyrrachium. Usually Caesar's men came off best but once his men were put to flight and he nearly lost his own camp; for when Pompey attacked, none of Caesar's men would stand and fight. The ditches were heaped up 15
with dead, and men were driven right back against the ramparts of their camp and killed. Caesar stood facing his troops as they ran and tried to turn them back but it was no good. Indeed, when he tried to grab hold of the standards, the standard bearers threw them away so that the enemy captured 32 of them. At one point Caesar was very nearly killed himself. A 20

tall, powerful man came running away past him and Caesar caught hold of him and ordered him to halt and face the enemy. The man was overcome with panic and lifted his sword to strike Caesar – but before he could do it Caesar's shield-bearer lopped off the man's arm at the shoulder.

Caesar thought that he was completely defeated, but Pompey – either because he was being over-careful or for some other reason – did not follow up the victory. Instead he recalled his men once they had forced the enemy back into their camp. 25

Caesar remarked to his friends, 'The enemy would have won today if their general were a winner!' Then he went by himself to his tent, where he lay down and spent a night of misery, thinking he was a failure as a general. 30

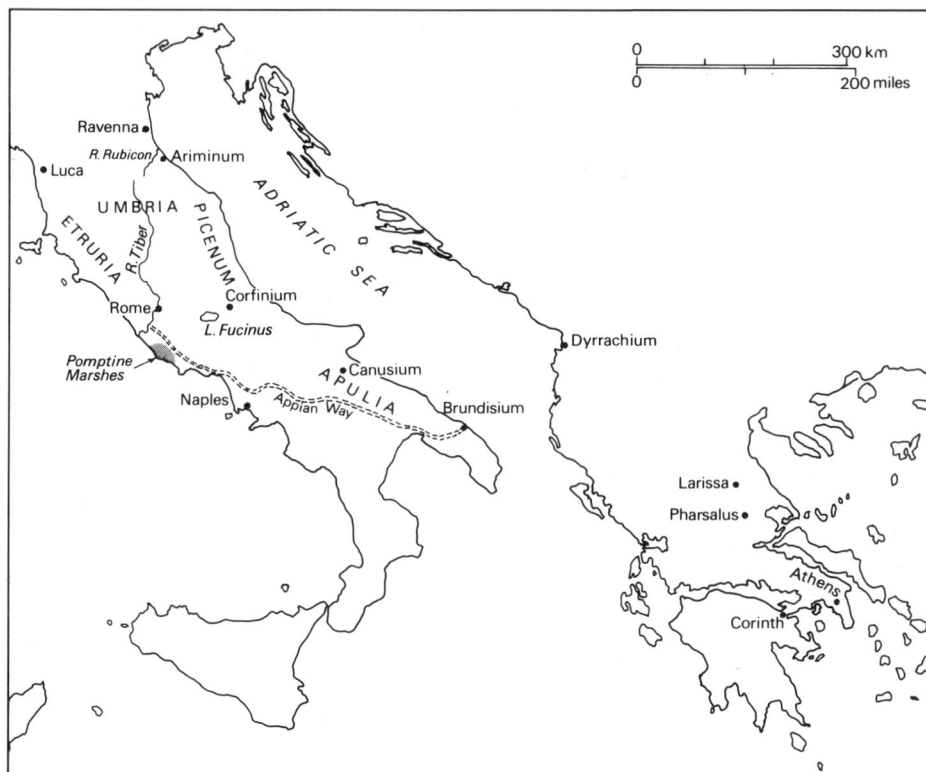

From Dyrrachium to Pharsalus

Caesar decided to leave that place where he was being defeated by lack of provisions and to move his armies to the rich and fertile cities of Thessaly and Macedonia. So, next morning, after tossing about on his couch all night with worry, he broke camp and set off. 35

Plut.
Pomp. 66 Pompey's followers were delighted with their victory at Dyrrachium, so they were eager to settle the war in one big battle. But Pompey was frightened to take the risk. He knew that Caesar's men had years of experience in winning battles and that they were impossible to defeat in a straight fight – but that when it came to the other aspects of war things 40

were different. They were all old men by now and were not up to long marches, changing camps, digging trenches and building walls. What they wanted was to come to close quarters as soon as possible and fight it out hand to hand. Pompey knew that his best plan was to tire them out by avoiding battle and letting them suffer hardships. 45

Plut. Caes. 41 No one agreed with him except Cato. This was because Cato wanted to spare the lives of his fellow citizens. Indeed, when he saw the thousand enemy dead after the battle of Dyrrachium he burst into tears, covered his face and hurried away.

Plut. Pomp. 67 Now Pompey set out after Caesar, still determined to avoid a battle but 50 to harrass him and keep him short of supplies. But as he followed behind Caesar in this quiet way, his own followers began to make noisy complaints against him. They said that he was really carrying on this war against the Fatherland and the senate, not against Caesar at all. They said that all he wanted was to be in power all the time and have the men who should really 55 be ruling the world running after him as his bodyguards and attendants. Domitius turned people against him by always calling him 'Agamemnon', or 'King of Kings'.

Now Pompey hated to be unpopular, nor could he bear to disappoint his friends, so this sort of talk – and there was a lot of it – forced him to 60 abandon his well thought-out plan – a thing which would be disgraceful for the captain of a ship to do, never mind a general in absolute command over so many nations and armies. When they marched down into the plain of Pharsalus, Pompey's friends forced him to hold a council of war.

Plut. Caes. 42 In fact they were so confident and so sure of victory that three of them 65 began to squabble about who should become Pontifex Maximus in place of Caesar. Many of them sent men to Rome to rent houses which would be grand enough for praetors and consuls – for they had no doubt that they would hold these positions after the war. But it was the cavalry, glittering in their splendid armour, with their sleek horses and their handsome good 70 looks who were really itching for battle. There were 7,000 of them against Caesar's 1,000. The numbers of the infantry were unequal too, for Pompey had 45,000 men and Caesar 22,000.

Plut. Pomp. 67 But they had forgotten that they were fighting against Caesar – Caesar who had taken 1,000 cities by storm, who had conquered over 300 nations, 75 who had fought more victorious battles with the Gauls and Germans than could be counted; Caesar who had captured a hundred times 10,000 prisoners and killed as many more as they ran before him defeated on the battlefield!

Plut. Pomp. 68 That night Pompey had a dream. He saw himself entering his theatre 80 and hanging up rich booty in the temple of Victorious Venus while the people clapped him. This dream cheered him up a little – but it worried him too, for he remembered that Caesar could trace his family back to Venus. Did the dream mean that he would make Caesar bright and glorious?

Appian Civil Wars 2.6.8 At midnight Caesar offered a sacrifice. He called upon Mars and the 85 goddess Venus, from whom he was descended. He made a vow that if all went well he would build her a temple in Rome to thank her as the Bringer of Victory. Then a bright light appeared in the sky. It shot from Caesar's camp towards Pompey's and then went out. Pompey's supporters said that it was a sign of a brilliant victory for them over their enemies; Caesar took 90 it as an omen that he would fall on the power of Pompey and extinguish it.

Plut.
Pomp. 68 The next morning Caesar began to break camp, intending to march his men on to Scotussa. The soldiers were already taking down the tents, and the pack-animals and camp attendants were going ahead when scouts came in to report that they had spied many shields moving to and fro in the 95 enemy camp and that they could hear the tramp of men coming out for battle. Soon more scouts arrived and reported that Pompey's front ranks were already taking up their battle positions. 'The time has come', said Caesar. 'Today we will fight against men, not against shortage and hunger'. Then he quickly gave orders for the purple tunic to be hung out in front of 100 his tent (this is the Roman battle signal). When the soldiers saw this they stopped taking down their tents and, with shouts of joy, ran to pick up their weapons. When the officers arranged them in battle order, they fell into line without fuss, like well-trained dancers.

IV.5 The battle of Pharsalus

Plut.
Pomp. 69 Pompey took charge of his right wing facing Mark Antony. In the centre he placed his father-in-law, Scipio, to face Lucius Calvinus. Domitius commanded the left wing supported by most of the cavalry, who had gathered here in order to attack Caesar himself and wipe out the Tenth Legion. This was generally reckoned to be the best fighting legion and 5 Caesar usually went into battle with it.

Plut.
Caes. 64 When Caesar saw where the cavalry were massing, he was worried by their huge numbers and magnificence. So he gave orders for six cohorts from the rear ranks to come up without being seen. He positioned them behind his right wing and gave them careful instructions. 10

Plut.
Brutus 5 It is also said that Caesar was worried about Brutus and ordered his officers not to kill him in the fighting. If he gave himself up they were to do him no harm, just take him prisoner. But if he put up a fight they were to leave him alone and not attack him. For there was a rumour that Brutus was Caesar's own son. 15

Plut.
Pomp. 71 Now the plain of Pharsalus was filled with warriors and horses and weapons and the battle signal had been hoisted by both sides.

Plut.
Caes. 44 As Caesar was about to move up his legionaries and go into action he noticed one of his centurions – a battle-hardened warrior – giving words of encouragement to the men under his command and urging them to try to 20 fight as well as he did himself. Caesar called to him by name, 'Gaius Crassinius! How do you think we'll get on today?' Crassinius stretched out his right hand and shouted at the top of his voice, 'We will win a glorious victory, Caesar, and by tonight you will have reason to praise me – be I alive or be I dead!' Then he turned and charged right into the enemy at a 25

run taking with him the 120 soldiers under his command. He cut his way through the first rank of the enemy killing men to right and left but as he pressed on he was stopped by a sword being thrust into his mouth – its point came out through the back of his neck.

And so the battle started.

Plut. *Caes.* 45 and *Pomp.* 69
When the infantry clashed together in the centre, Pompey's cavalry rode proudly up from the wing to surround the enemy's right, but just as they were about to attack, Caesar's six hidden cohorts sprang out. They did not throw their javelins, which was what they usually did, nor did they stab at the thighs and legs of the horsemen. Instead they went for their eyes and faces, for this is what Caesar had told them to do. He knew these young men, who knew nothing of wars and wounds, were very proud of their good looks and would dread such wounds not only because of the pain they would cause, but also because of the ugliness they would leave.

And he was right! They could not stand the javelins stabbing up at them but turned their heads and covered their faces. In the end, in complete confusion they turned and fled disgracefully and so ruined everything, for the cohorts who had driven them off now ran behind Pompey's infantry, attacking them in the rear, and began to cut them down.

Plut. *Caes.* 46
When Caesar reached the ramparts of Pompey's camp and saw his enemies lying dead or still being killed, he groaned and said, 'They asked for it! In spite of all my conquests they would have destroyed me in the law courts if I had disbanded my army.'

For most of those who were captured alive Caesar found places in his own legions. Many of their leading men he let go free. One of these was Brutus, the man who was to kill him.

IV. 6 Pompey's escape

Plut. *Pomp.* 72
Pompey saw his infantry running away and when he noticed the cloud of dust he guessed what had happened to his cavalry. It is hard to say what thoughts flashed though his head – but he looked crazy, like a man out of his mind. He completely forgot that he was Pompey the Great and without saying a word to anyone he walked slowly back to his camp. He went into his tent and sat down without saying a word until his fleeing troops came pouring into the camp with the enemy hot on their heels, and then all he could say was 'What? Even in the camp?' Then saying no more he changed into clothes more suitable for his new position and slipped away.

The rest of his legions fled too, and there was dreadful slaughter in the camp as all the tent guards and camp servants were cut down.

When Caesar's soldiers finally captured the camp they saw everywhere signs of foolishness and frivolity. Every tent was wreathed about with boughs of myrtle and inside were couches heaped with flowers, tables covered with drinking goblets, and bowls of wine laid everywhere. It looked as though it had all been prepared for men who were going to celebrate after a sacrifice, not for men buckling on armour for a battle.

Plut.
Pomp. 73 Pompey left the camp on horseback with a few followers. After a short while, since there was no pursuit, he let the reins fall loose from his hands and ambled quietly away. Through his mind went the thoughts you would expect in a man who for 34 years had always been a conqueror and a master, and who now in his old age for the first time was finding out about being a defeated man and a fugitive. He thought how in a single hour he had lost the power and the glory which he had won in so many wars and battles. He thought how, a little time ago, he was guarded by huge armies of foot soldiers and cavalry, while now he was slipping away unnoticed by his pursuers and quite unimportant.

    He by-passed the city of Larissa and came to the Vale of Tempe. Being thirsty he threw himself down and drank from the river. Then he got up and travelled on down the valley until he came to the sea where he spent the rest of the night in a fisherman's shack. When dawn broke he went aboard a river-boat. He allowed only freemen to board the boat with him; his slaves he ordered not to be afraid but to go back and surrender to Caesar. Then in this boat he travelled along the coast until he saw a good-sized merchant ship which was about to put to sea.

Plut.
Pomp. 76   So Pompey sailed away. First he followed the coast and then crossed over to Mytilene to collect his wife Cornelia and his son. Then, since Caesar was pursuing him, he travelled on, putting in at harbours only when he needed food and water. He was afraid of his enemy's speed, and so he began to look for somewhere to hide for the time being. He decided to retreat to Egypt. With his wife he set sail from Cyprus on a trireme and crossed the seas in safety. His friends followed him, some in war-galleys like his own, some in cargo-ships. When he heard that Ptolemy the king of Egypt was at Pelusium waging war against his sister, Pompey decided to go to him there. He sent a messenger ahead to announce his arrival and to ask the king's help.

IV.7 'Dead men don't bite'

Plut.
Pomp. 77 Now King Ptolemy was very young and his affairs were really run by the eunuch Potheinus. This Potheinus called a meeting of the most eminent men of Egypt (they were only eminent because he made them so) and he asked them what they thought should be done about Pompey. It was a dreadful thing that the fate of Pompey the Great should be decided by the eunuch Potheinus, Theodotus of Chios who was a teacher of rhetoric, and Achillas the Egyptian – for these were the king's chief advisers. This was the court whose decision Pompey the Great awaited as he tossed about at anchor not far from the shore. Some of the advisers said that Pompey should be driven away, some said that he should be made welcome. Then Theodotus spoke using all his skill and power and said, 'We must do neither. If we make Pompey welcome Caesar will become our enemy and Pompey will be our master. If we drive him away, Pompey will be our

enemy and Caesar will hate us for making him continue his hunt. The best thing to do is to invite the fellow ashore – and kill him! Caesar will be pleased and Pompey will be harmless.' Then (we are told) he smiled and added the words 'Dead men don't bite.'

Plut. *Pomp.* 78 The plan was agreed on and Achillas was given the job of carrying it out. He took with him a man called Septimius, who had once served as an officer under Pompey, a centurion called Salvius and three or four slaves. They climbed into a small boat and set out for Pompey's ship.

By this time all the most important people from the other ships which had sailed with Pompey had joined him aboard his vessel to find out what was going on. When they saw that Pompey was not being welcomed with the usual royal pomp and splendour but by a few men sailing up in a single fishing boat, they were very suspicious at such a lack of respect. They advised Pompey to give orders for his ship to be rowed back to the open sea while they were still out of catapult range. But by this time the fishing boat was alongside. Septimius stood up first and shouted up to Pompey in the language of the Romans calling him 'Imperator'. Next Achillas welcomed him in Greek and invited him aboard saying, 'This part of the sea is full of sandbanks and is too shallow to float your trireme'. As he was speaking the men on deck could see that the crews were hurrying aboard Ptolemy's warships and heavy-armed troops were forming up on the beach. There seemed to be no chance of escape even if they changed their minds; besides if they hesitated it might give an excuse for murdering them.

So Pompey hugged Cornelia who by now was wailing for him as though he were already dead, and ordered two centurions to climb down into the boat ahead of him. He also sent down one of his freedmen called Philip and a slave called Scythes. Achillas held out a hand to help Pompey down but before taking it he paused, and turning to his wife and son he spoke the words of the poet Sophocles:

'In the house of a king
Even a freeman is a slave.'

Plut. *Pomp.* 79 These were the last words he said to his friends; then he climbed into the boat.

It was a long way from the trireme to the shore but no one in the boat said a friendly word to him; so, to make conversation, he looked at Septimius and said 'If I'm not mistaken, you are an old comrade of mine!' Septimius just nodded without saying a word or giving any sign of friendship. A deep silence fell on them all. Pompey then took out a little scroll and began to read it over. It was a speech which he had written in Greek to use when he spoke to Ptolemy.

From the trireme Cornelia and the others watched the fishing boat as it came closer to the beach. At first she was extremely worried but when she saw the king's men lining up at the point where the boat would reach the shore she was much relieved, for she thought that they were a guard of honour.

Just then Pompey stood up ready for landing and clutched Philip's hand to steady himself. Septimius ran him through from behind with a sword,

then Salvius and Achillas in turn drew their daggers and stabbed him. 60
Pompey neither did nor said anything that was unworthy. He pulled his
toga over his face with both hands, groaned, and surrendered himself to
the blows.

He was one year short of sixty and ended his life only one day after his 48 B.C.
birthday. 65

Plut.
Pomp. 80 When the people aboard the ships saw the murder they raised cries and
wails that could be heard even from the shore. Quickly they raised their
anchors and fled. A fresh wind helped them as they made for the open sea
so the Egyptians gave up hope of catching them and turned back.

They cut off the head of Pompey the Great, and the rest of his body they 70
threw naked out of the boat and left it – a sad sight for those who came to
gawp. Philip stayed beside the body until they had feasted their eyes, then
he washed it in the tide, and wrapped one of his own tunics round it. He
did not have what he needed so he searched along the beach until he found
the wreckage of a little fishing boat. It was old but it would do to make a 75
funeral pyre good enough for a naked, mutilated corpse.

As he was gathering the pieces of wood and building the pyre an old man
walked up. He was a Roman and as a youngster he had served his first
campaigns under Pompey. He called to Philip, 'Who do you think you are,
fellow, organising the funeral of Pompey the Great?' Philip explained that 80
he was a freedman of Pompey and the old Roman then said, 'Look here,
you can't have this honour all to yourself. Let me share it with you. I will
not regret my life as an exile on this foreign land so bitterly if, to balance all
my sufferings, I am given this happiness at last – to touch with my hands
and prepare for burial the greatest Imperator of the Romans.' 85

Denarius issued in
Spain in 46–45 B.C.
(F. is short for 'filius' –
the Latin word for
'son'.)

V Caesar's last years

V.1 The war continues

Plut. *Caes.* 48 Caesar arrived in Alexandria just after Pompey's death. When Theodotus came to him bringing him Pompey's head, he turned away shuddering and when he was given Pompey's signet ring he burst into tears. Achillas and Potheinus the eunuch he put to death but Theodotus escaped. He fled from Egypt and lived a wandering life, miserable and hated. 5

It was while he was in Egypt that Caesar met Cleopatra. Plutarch says that Cleopatra's beauty would not astound anyone who saw her. She attracted people by her charming manner, brilliant conversation and stimulating personality. At that time she was about 21 years old and was fighting a war against her brother King Ptolemy. Caesar was charmed by her, and before he left he defeated her 10 brother and her other enemies and made her queen of all Egypt. A little later she had a baby. He was said to be Caesar's son and people called him Caesarion.

From Alexandria, Caesar went to Pontus where the son of Mithridates had 47 B.C. seized the opportunity to make war.

Suet. *Caes.* 35 Caesar defeated him in a single battle, four hours after catching sight of 15 him and within five days of his arrival in the country. He afterwards made a number of remarks about Pompey, saying how lucky he had been to gain much of his reputation as a soldier by defeating such a feeble kind of enemy.

Plut. *Caes.* 51 After this he crossed to Italy and went to Rome. It was December and 20 Caesar had been dictator for a whole year. For the next year he was proclaimed consul.

V.2 The death of Cato

After the battle of Pharsalus, Cato and Scipio escaped to Africa, where they gathered a large force of soldiers. Caesar decided to make an expedition against them. He moved at incredible speed and defeated Scipio in the battle of Thapsus.

Cato took no part in this battle since he was guarding the city of Utica. Caesar was eager to take Cato alive, so he hurried on to Utica with all possible speed. 5

But Cato had made up his mind a long time before this that he would commit suicide. He spent the night making sure that the others were going to be safe – either by surrendering to Caesar or escaping by sea.

Plut. *Cato the Younger* 70 As the birds were beginning to sing, Cato fell asleep for a short time. His freedman Butas came in and told him that the harbours were very quiet. 10 Cato told him to close the door; then he lay down on his couch as if he was going to rest there for what remained of the night.

After Butas had gone, Cato drew his sword and stabbed himself in the chest. His hand, however, was inflamed, and his thrust was too light to

Roman denarius issued in 32 B.C., showing the head of Cleopatra.

Denarius issued in Africa in 47–46 B.C. PRO.PR is an abbreviation of Pro Praetore – the title of the governor of a province. The name M(arcus) CATO is very faint.

finish himself off at once. He fell over in his struggle to die and made so 15
much noise that his son came running in with his friends. They saw that he
was smothered in blood and that most of his bowels were sticking out; but
he was still alive and his eyes were still open. They were all appalled at the
sight. The doctor went up to him and tried to replace his bowels (which
were still uninjured) and to stitch up the wound. When Cato recovered, he 20
realised what had happened. Pushing the doctor away, he tore at his bowels
with his hand. The wound was opened afresh and death soon followed.

Plut.
Caes. 54
When Caesar learned that Cato had committed suicide, he was clearly
annoyed, though the reason for this is uncertain. At any rate, what he said
was, 'Cato, I begrudge you your death, just as you begrudged me the 25
chance to save your life.'

V.3 I came: I saw: I conquered

On his return to Rome Caesar held four triumphs in a single month. They were to
celebrate his victories in Gaul, Alexandria, Pontus and Africa.

Suet.
Caes. 37
The first and most magnificent was his triumph over the Gauls. As he rode
his chariot along the Velabrum, the axle broke and he was nearly thrown
out. He climbed up the Capitol by torchlight with forty elephants carrying 5
lanterns lining the route to left and right.

In their usual way, the soldiers who followed his chariot sang songs and
joked about their general.

Suet.
Caes. 51, 49
'Hide your wives, you Roman husbands,
The baldy lady killer's home! 10
He's spent his gold in Gaul on girlies,
The gold you gave him here in Rome!'

Suet.
Caes. 37
In his triumph over Pontus on one of the placards used to describe the
war, were written just three words:
VENI   VIDI   VICI 15

Suet.
Caes. 38
To each of his veteran infantrymen he gave as booty 24,000 sestertii and
also plots of land to farm. To every Roman he gave 10 modii of grain and
10 pounds of oil. He promised everyone 300 sestertii and when there was a
delay in handing it out he added an extra 100.

Weights and measures

1 Roman pound	= 327 grams
	= 0.721 English pound
	= approximately 12 ounces
1 modius	= 16 sextarii
	= 16 × 0.546 litres
	= approx. 9 litres or 2 gallons

He gave a banquet, distributed meat to everyone and provided all sorts 20
of entertainments. He put on gladiatorial fights and plays in every district
of the city. The plays were performed by actors speaking many different
languages. There were races too in the Circus, athletic displays and a mock
sea-battle. For the races the Circus was lengthened at both ends and the
track was surrounded by a water ditch. 25

A flood of people came surging to these shows from every direction.
Visitors pitched tents in the alley-ways and streets of the city and the
crowds were so great that many people were crushed to death. Amongst
them were two senators.

Aerial photograph of the Circus Maximus. The starting boxes were on the right and races consisted of seven circuits of the central 'spine'.

V.4   The fifth triumph

Plut.
Caes. 56   When all this was done Caesar was elected consul for the fourth time and
he set out for Spain to fight against the sons of Pompey. He killed 30,000 of
the enemy, but lost 1,000 of his best troops. Pompey's younger son
escaped, but one of Caesar's officers brought him the elder son's head. This
was Caesar's last war. After it he held another triumph, but this disturbed 5
the Romans very deeply for it was not a triumph over foreign generals and
barbarian kings. It was to celebrate the wiping out of the family and
children of the mightiest of the Romans.

Suet.   After his Spanish triumph, he gave
Caes. 38   the people two dinners – for when he   10
saw what was being served up for the
first one he thought that there was not
enough and that it made him look mean.
He gave the second five days later and
it was much more luxurious.   15

The coin is a denarius issued by Pompey's son Sextus in 44–43 B.C.
'Neptuni' is the Latin way of saying 'Of Neptune' or 'Neptune's own'.

A better place to live?

Suet.
Caes. 44

In Rome, Caesar's projects grew more and more ambitious day by day. He wanted to improve the appearance of the city and make it a better place to live. Equally he wanted to protect and extend the power of Rome.

The Temple of Mother Venus and Caesar's Forum, in ancient times and today.

Three of the temple columns have been reconstructed from the ruins. 'Caesar built the Temple of Mother Venus as he had vowed to do before the battle of Pharsalus. He also built a precinct around the temple as a forum for the Roman people. By the side of the goddess he put a beautiful statue of Cleopatra.' (Appian, *Civil Wars*, II.102)

Pliny the Elder tells us that Caesar gave 100 million sestertii just for the site on which his forum was built.

The calendar

One of Caesar's most lasting acts was to reorganise the Roman calendar. His system, with a few minor alterations, is the one we still use today.

The old system

For hundreds of years the Roman calendar had consisted of twelve months based on the movements of the moon. Plutarch says that this system dated back to Numa, the second king of Rome.

Plut.
Numa 18
Numa realised that this would make the year eleven days too short to fit in with the movements of the sun, so every second year he added an extra 'intercalary' month of twenty-two days. The Romans called this month 'Mercedinus' and it was fitted into the calendar after February.

The new system

By Caesar's time the calendar was in complete confusion. It seems that politicians had been able to persuade the priests to add an extra month even when it was not necesary so that they could prolong their year of office.

Suet.
Caes. 40
Caesar reformed the calendar which the priests had got into such a mess. (They had the privilege of adding an extra month when they liked but by now the harvest was not being celebrated in the summer, nor the vintage in the autumn.)

Caesar made the year 365 days long to fit the sun's course. He abolished the intercalary month and added one day every fourth year. He wanted the new year to start according to the right season, so he added two extra months between November and December. So it was that in the year in which Caesar did all this there were fifteen months – because one had already been added according to the old system.

46 B.C.

Suet.
Caes. 42 and 43
Many people were hoping that he would cancel all debts, but they were disappointed. Instead he made an arrangement whereby debts were reduced by about one quarter. He was very careful and very strict in the administration of justice, and dismissed many senators convicted of extortion.

In particular he enforced the law against extravagance. His watchmen, who were placed in various parts of the market, used to seize any delicacies which were on sale illegally and take them to him. Sometimes he sent out his lictors and soldiers into people's dining-rooms with orders to take anything which had escaped the eyes of his watchmen – even if it had already been served up at table.

above: An artist's reconstruction of the Basilica Iulia. (The two columns at the front were added later.) This basilica became the most important law-court in Rome, but Caesar did not live to see it completed.

The Basilica Iulia today. (The three large columns in the middle distance belong to the Temple of Castor, and the smaller building on the left of them is the Temple of Vesta. The arch in the background belongs to a later period. It was erected to celebrate the capture of Jerusalem by the Emperor Titus in 70 A.D.)

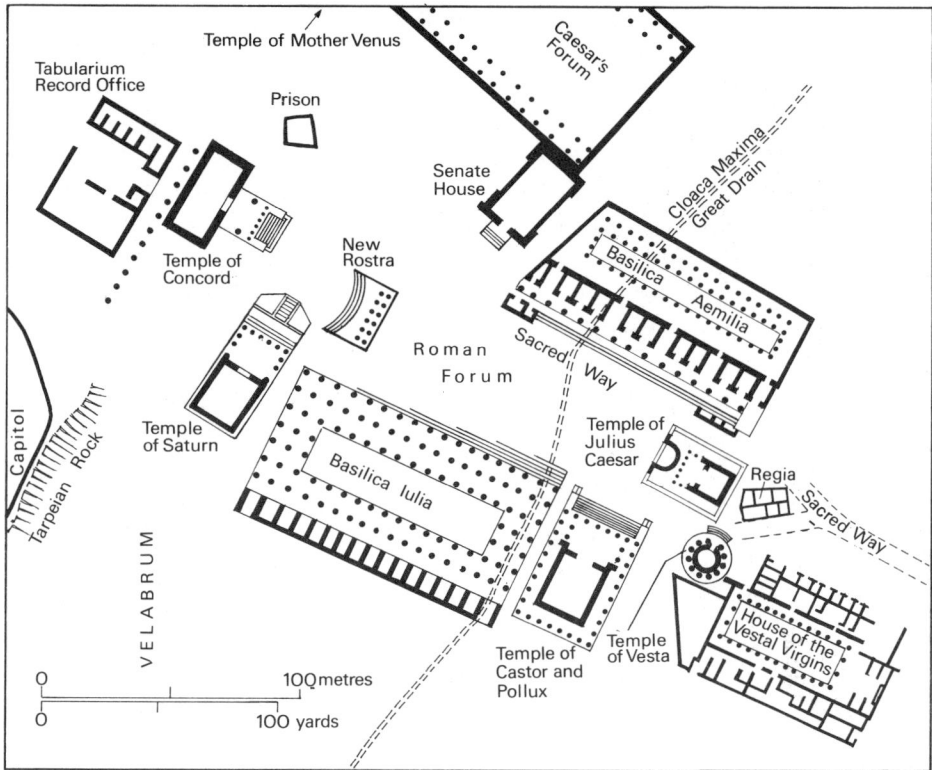

Map labels: Temple of Mother Venus, Caesar's Forum, Tabularium Record Office, Prison, Senate House, Cloaca Maxima Great Drain, Basilica Aemilia, Temple of Concord, New Rostra, Roman Forum, Sacred Way, Capitol Tarpeian Rock, Temple of Saturn, Basilica Iulia, Temple of Julius Caesar, Regia, Sacred Way, VELABRUM, Temple of Castor and Pollux, Temple of Vesta, House of the Vestal Virgins

0 ____ 100 metres
0 ____ 100 yards

Suet. *Caesar* 41, 42, 76 and 80

He made a census of the people, street by street, and reduced the number who received grain at public expense from 320,000 to 150,000. 35

He admitted to the senate people to whom he had given citizenship, and some half-civilised Gauls. A poster appeared saying, 'Long live the Republic! Let no one show the new senators where the senate house is.' People made up songs saying that one minute the Gauls had been captives in Caesar's triumph and the next minute he had made them senators. 40 Another one was about the Gauls taking their trousers off – and putting on the purple-edged toga.

Suet. *Caes.* 44

He intended to drain and level the lake where he had presented the sea battle, and construct the world's largest temple to Mars. Next he intended to build an enormous theatre sloping down from the Tarpeian Rock; then 45 to reduce all the books of civil law down to a reasonable size (keeping the best and most important laws) and to open to the public the biggest possible libraries of Greek and Roman books. He also planned to drain the Pomptine marshes, let the water out of Lake Fucinus, build a highway from the Adriatic to the Tiber right over the Apenines and to cut a canal 50 through the Isthmus of Corinth. He also planned new wars – one against the Dacians who had invaded Roman territory, and one against the Parthians. All of these activities and plans were cut short by his death.

V.5 Dictator for ever

Suet.
Caes. 76

In spite of all this, Caesar said and did things which tipped the scale against him so that men thought that he used his power wrongly and that it was right to slay him. He became permanent consul, dictator for ever and censor of public morals. He took as a new first name the title 'Imperator' and as another name the title 'Parens Patriae' – Father of the Fatherland. 5
He had his statue set up amongst the statues of the kings and a special grandstand built for him to sit in at the theatre, and he received honours too magnificent for a mortal man – he had a golden throne in the senate house and one in the law courts: there was a holy chariot and litter to carry his statue in the procession of the gods in the Circus: temples were built in 10 his honour, altars set up, his statue stood amongst those of the gods, he was given a holy couch and a priest, and one of the months of the year was named after him.

Plut.
Caes. 60, 61

But what made people really hate him and wish him dead was his eagerness to become king. 15

There was for example his insult to the tribunes. It was the festival of the Lupercalia, when many young men of noble families and many of the magistrates run up and down through the city naked. They cause a great deal of laughter and enjoyment by hitting everyone they meet with hairy leather whips. Many women of high rank purposely stand in their way and 20 hold out their hands like children at school to be slapped. They think this will help to make the birth of their children easier if they are pregnant, or help them to become pregnant if they are childless.

Caesar was watching all this as he sat on a golden throne, dressed in his triumphal finery. One of the men running in the sacred race was the consul 25 Mark Antony. He came sprinting into the Forum carrying a diadem wreathed with laurel. The crowd made way for him and he held out the diadem for Caesar to take. A few men in the crowd who had been put up to it began to clap but very few others joined in. However, when Caesar refused to take the crown, everybody applauded. Antony offered the 30 diadem a second time and again the same few people clapped, but when Caesar refused the diadem again the whole crowd applauded.

This had all been an experiment and it had failed. Caesar rose from his seat and ordered the diadem to be taken to the Capitol to be offered to Jupiter, Best and Greatest. 35

Plut. *Caes.* 61 and
Suet. *Caes.* 79

People also noticed that Caesar's statues had been crowned with royal diadems. Two of the tribunes, Flavius and Marullus, went up to them and pulled down these crowns; then they arrested the men who had first hailed Caesar as king and led them off to prison. The people followed, with cheers, calling the tribunes Brutuses, for Brutus was the man who had 40 destroyed the power of the kings at Rome, taking the power from one man and giving it to the senate and the people. This made Caesar angry. He deprived Marullus and Flavius of their tribuneship and made a speech against them in which he included many insults against the people. There

Denarius of Julius Caesar. The other side shows Venus and a winged statue of Victory.

were two possible reasons for Caesar's annoyance. He himself said that he wanted the opportunity to remove the crowns himself, and get the credit for doing so. On the other hand he may have hoped that this hint of royal power would have been received more favourably.

V.6   Marcus Brutus

Plut. *Caes.* 62
Brutus 6

As a result of all this the people generally began to think about Marcus Brutus who was descended from the famous Brutus of old and who was the son-in-law of Cato.

Brutus was a grave and serious man. It was not easy to make him do things out of favouritism; instead he let himself be guided by reasoned arguments and always acted in the most honourable way. This gave him great power and success in whatever he did. No one could flatter him into supporting an unjust cause. Some men find it impossible to resist when people nag and nag shamelessly at them to do something. Brutus thought that to give in to this was disgraceful for a great man.

Those who wanted to remove Caesar and thought that Brutus was the most likely man to do it for them did not dare to speak to him directly. But under cover of night they covered the praetor's tribunal and the chair on which Brutus sat, with written messages. They said such things as, 'You are asleep, Brutus', or 'You are no true Brutus.'

A denarius issued by Brutus either in 59 B.C. (in opposition to the 'three headed monster') or in 55–54 B.C. (when there was a rumour that Pompey was aiming for sole power).

V.7   Cassius

Plut.
Brutus 9, 10

Brutus had a relative called Cassius. From his earliest days Cassius had bitterly hated all kings and tyrants. When he was a boy, he went to the same school as Faustus, the son of Sulla. Once Faustus was bragging to the other boys about his father's absolute power. Cassius jumped on him and beat him up. Faustus' guardians and relatives wanted to bring the matter to court, but Pompey would not allow it. Instead he brought the two boys together and asked them what had happened. We are told that young Cassius said,

'Come on Faustus, say in front of him what you said to make me angry – if you dare – and I will smash your face again!'

This was the sort of man Cassius was. Now when Cassius tried to persuade his friends to join a conspiracy against Caesar, they all agreed to join, provided that Brutus would be their leader. They pointed out that it was not only force of numbers, determination and courage they needed, but the reputation of a man such as Brutus. His presence would make the victim acceptable so to speak, and show that Brutus would not have joined the plot if it had been dishonourable.

Cassius thought this over and then went to see Brutus. He asked him if he intended to go to the meeting of the senate on the Ides of March.

'I have heard rumours', he said, 'that Caesar's friends will try to declare him king on that day'.

A denarius issued c. 62–56 B.C. by Faustus to commemorate one of his father's victories. Sulla liked to think of himself as 'felix' – blessed by the Gods.

5

10

15

5

10

15

20

Brutus answered that he would not go to the meeting.

'But what if you are ordered to go?'

'Then it would be my duty to speak out in defence of my country and to die for liberty'. 25

Cassius was encouraged by this and said, 'But what Roman will let you die defending liberty? Do you not know who you are, Brutus? Do you think that those messages were put on your tribunal by weavers and the scum of the market stalls? No, they were put there by the most eminent and important citizens. They expect the other praetors to give them gifts 30 and shows and gladiatorial fights; but they look to you to free them from tyranny. You owe it to your ancestors. These citizens are ready to face anything to support you, if you prove you are the man they think you are.' After this he put his arms round Brutus and embraced him, and they went off together to join their friends. 35

The reverse of the coin shown in V.6. It refers to Brutus' famous ancestor of the same name.

V.8   The wife of Brutus

Plut.
Brutus 13

Brutus realised the danger involved. In public he tried to keep his thoughts to himself and give nothing away; but at home, and especially at night, he was not the same man. Sometimes his thoughts woke him up when he wanted to sleep, and it was impossible to keep things from his wife, Porcia, who slept by his side. 5

Porcia was an affectionate woman who loved her husband dearly. She was full of spirit and common sense, and did not try to question her husband about his secrets until she had put herself to the following test.

She took a little knife – the sort that barbers use to cut finger nails – and, having sent her maids out of the room, gave herself a deep gash on the 10 thigh. She lost a lot of blood, so that the wound soon gave her a lot of pain and a feverish shivering. When the pain was at its height she went to speak to her husband.

'Brutus', she said, 'I am Cato's daughter. I wasn't given to you just to share your bed and board like some concubine. I should be your true 15 partner, both in your joys and in your sorrows. You have been a perfect husband to me, but how can I prove my love to you? You won't share your troubles with me – but when you're so worried you need someone to confide in. I know they say that women are too weak to be trusted with secrets, but I come from a great family and keep the best of company. 20 Surely that counts for something?

'I am lucky enough to be the daughter of Cato and the wife of Brutus. I had never realised how confident this could make me feel; now I know that I am even superior to pain.'

Having said this, she showed him her wound and described her test. 25 Brutus was amazed; he raised his hands to heaven and prayed that the gods would make him successful and help him show that he was worthy to be Porcia's husband. Then he set about bringing his wife back to health.

When the day came, Brutus set out from his house. His wife was the only one who knew that he was wearing a dagger.

30

V.9   The Ides of March

Plut.
Brutus 14

A meeting of the senate had been called and Caesar was expected to attend. The conspirators decided that this was their chance for they would all be able to be there without arousing suspicion. Furthermore, all the most important people in the state would be present and the conspirators hoped that as soon as these men saw what was happening they would join in and and strike for liberty. There was another point too. The room in which the senate was to meet seemed to have been chosen by fate. It was in the portico of the beautiful theatre which Pompey had built on the Field of Mars. In the room there was a statue of Pompey which the citizens had set up in his honour. The senate had been summoned to meet here in the middle of March on the day which the Romans call 'the Ides of March'.

5

10

Suet.
Caes. 81

Clear omens were given that Caesar would be murdered. Once when he was sacrificing, the haruspex, a man called Spurinna, told him to beware of a danger that he would meet between that day and the Ides of March. On the day before the Ides of March a wren – the Romans called it the 'little kingbird' – flew into the meeting-room at the theatre of Pompey, carrying with it a sprig of laurel. A flock of other birds of all sorts came flying after it and tore it to pieces in the room.

15

Plut.
Caes. 63

The night before the meeting, while Caesar was sleeping as usual beside, his wife, Calpurnia, all the doors and windows of the house suddenly burst open. Caesar woke startled by the din. Then he noticed Calpurnia who was still slumbering deeply was mumbling incoherently and groaning. When she woke she told him that she had been dreaming and that in her dream she was holding his murdered corpse in her arms.

20

When morning came she begged him not to go out but to postpone the meeting of the senate. She pleaded with him to try the other methods of finding out the future if he did not believe her dream. It seemed that even Caesar was nervous by this time, for he knew that Calpurnia was not superstitious like most women and he could see that she was very upset. The haruspices now made a large number of sacrifices – but every omen was bad. So Caesar decided to send Antony to dismiss the senate.

25

30

Plut.
Caes. 64

Just then Decimus Brutus arrived. Caesar trusted this man so completely that he had made him the second heir in his will, but he was in the plot with Cassius and the other Brutus. Decimus Brutus was worried that if Caesar did not come on that day the plot would be discovered, so he made fun of the haruspices. He said,

35

'Don't give those senators a chance to complain or make them feel fools. They are all ready to vote you the right to be called king of the provinces outside Italy and to wear the diadem wherever you go by land or sea. What do you think they'll say if I tell them to go away and come back when

40

Calpurnia has had some nicer dreams? You can imagine what your enemies would say. And who would listen to us when we tried to tell them that you don't think you're the king and they are the slaves? But if you really feel today is ill-omened, why not go along and tell them yourself and then postpone the meeting?' As he was speaking he had taken Caesar's arm and had begun to lead him along. 45

Plut. *Caes.* 63 On the way to the senate Caesar saw the haruspex Spurinna in the crowd. He called to him jokingly,

'Well, Spurinna, the Ides of March have come!'

The haruspex answered in a quiet voice, 'Yes, they've come – but they haven't yet gone'. 50

Plut. *Caes.* 65 There was also a man in the crowd called Artemidorus. He was a teacher of Greek philosophy and had come to know some of Brutus' friends well and so had found out a great deal about their plot. He had written down details of it in a small scroll which he meant to give to Caesar. But when he 55 saw that Caesar was giving all the scrolls handed to him by the people to his attendants, he got as close as possible and said,

'Read this one yourself, Caesar! Quickly! It's very important! It concerns you personally.' Caesar took the scroll, but every time he tried to read it someone else would call to him from the crowd, so, still holding it in his 60 hand unread, Caesar went into the meeting-place.

Plut. *Antony* 13, *Caesar* 66 and *Brutus* 17 Antony, the consul, was with Caesar. He was one of Caesar's real friends and he was a hefty, powerful man. The conspirators were worried about him and did not want him present at the assassination. They had talked of killing Antony at the same time as Caesar but Brutus had said no. 65

'If we are going to kill Caesar for the sake of the law and of justice, we must make sure that we do nothing unjust.'

So it was that Decimus Brutus stopped Antony outside the meeting-room and started a long conversation with him.

V.10   The sacrifice begins

Plut. *Brutus* 17 and Suet. *Caes.* 72 When Caesar entered the room all the senators stood up in his honour. Then he sat down and all the senators who were in the plot came and stood about his chair as if to pay their respects. Tillius Cimber made the first move. He went close to Caesar as though he was going to ask him a special favour. Caesar shook his head and waved Cimber away telling him to come 5 back later. Then it happened. Cimber gripped Caesar's toga at the shoulders. Caesar shouted 'Let go!' but as he turned one of the Casca brothers stabbed him just below the throat. Caesar grabbed Casca's arm and dug his stylus into it. Then as he struggled to his feet, he was stopped by another wound. 10

Plut. *Caes.* 66 That was how it began. The senators who knew nothing of the plot shook with terror when they saw what was happening. They did not dare to run away or to come to Caesar's help or even to raise a shout. Those who had come ready for the murder pulled out their naked daggers and clustered round Caesar. Wherever he looked he saw iron blades stabbing at his face and eyes. He was tangled like a wild animal in their hands – for they all had to have a hand in this murderous sacrifice. This is why Brutus struck him a blow. He stabbed him in the groin.

It is said that although Caesar defended himself against the others, leaping backwards and forwards shouting out in protest, when he saw that Brutus had a dagger too, he called to him in Greek 'You too, my son?'. Then pulling his toga over his head he sank down. It might have been by accident – or the murderers might have pushed him there – but when he fell it was against the pedestal of Pompey's statue. It was covered with blood. It looked as though Pompey himself had come to watch over this vengeance on his enemy. So Caesar lay at Pompey's feet, his body jerking with all those wounds. It is said that there were twenty-three of them. Many of the conspirators had cut each other as they struggled to stab him; Brutus was wounded in the hand.

Plut.
Caes. 69

Caesar was 56 years old when he died, and had outlived Pompey by little over four years. His mighty Guardian Spirit had looked after him when he was alive and was looking for vengeance now that he was dead. It would track down his murderers through every land and on every sea until not one of them was left and everyone who had a hand in the plot was punished.

There were many signs given by the gods to mark his death. For example, for seven nights after the murder a great comet blazed brilliantly in the night sky then disappeared. The sun's rays grew gloomy and all that year its disc rose pale and sickly giving no warmth, so that the air was dark and heavy round the earth, and fruits could not ripen but shrivelled with the cold and fell.

V.11   Dead, but not buried

Plut.
Brutus 18

Brutus now stepped to the centre of the room to explain what had been done and to tell the other senators not to be afraid, but they were so terrified that they turned and ran and got tangled and jammed in the doorway even though nobody was after them. Actually, it had been agreed that nobody else should be killed but that everyone should be given the chance to share in this new liberty.

Plut.
Caes. 67

When the senators came bursting out and fled down the streets the people who saw them were panic-stricken. Some of them locked themselves in their houses, others left their counters and shops and ran in to see what had happened – then they came running out again. Antony and Lepidus, Caesar's closest friends, slipped away and hid in the houses of friends. In fact Antony threw off his senator's toga and escaped disguised as a slave.

Brutus and his supporters on the other hand walked out of the meeting room together and marched up to the Capitol. Still hot from the murder, they waved their bare daggers. They were smiling and confident, not at all like people who wanted to escape. They kept calling to the crowd,

'Liberty! We're all free now!' And whenever they saw someone from a noble family they called 'Come and join us'.

Plut.
Brutus 18 At first people kept shouting in terror and milling about, but when they realised that no one else was being killed and that there was no looting, the senators and many of the common people calmed down and began to follow Brutus and his men up to the Capitol. There they gathered in a large crowd. Brutus spoke to them all very persuasively explaining what had happened.

When he finished, the crowd applauded and shouted to him to come down from the Capitol. This made the conspirators feel that the danger was over so they made their way to the Forum. The other conspirators walked in a group but Brutus was surrounded by crowds of the most important citizens who escorted him down from the stronghold in great honour and set him upon the rostra to speak to the common people. Before him was a huge crowd. They were a mixed bunch quite likely to burst into violent riot. However, when they saw Brutus they were overcome with awe and waited in respectful silence for him to speak. They listened attentively to all that he said and made no interruptions, but when Cinna, one of the other conspirators, began to speak, it was clear that not everyone in the crowd was happy about what had happened. For when Cinna began to criticise Caesar the crowd's anger blazed up. Violent abuse was shouted at Cinna, and the conspirators were forced to retreat again to the Capitol. When they arrived there Brutus, realising that there might be a siege, sent away the most eminent men who had come with him, for he thought it wrong that they should share his danger when they did not share his responsibility for the deed.

Plut.
Brutus 19 Next day the senate held a meeting in the Temple of Tellus, the goddess Earth. Antony and Cicero made speeches recommending a general amnesty and concord. A vote was taken and they decided not only that no action should be taken against the conspirators, but also that the consuls should ask the people to award them honours. After passing these decrees the senate broke up.

Now Antony sent his son up to the Capitol as a hostage and Brutus and the others came down once again. Both sides greeted each other heartily. Antony took Cassius home for dinner and Lepidus took Brutus. All the rest were looked after in the same friendly way.

Early next day the senate met again. First they gave a vote of thanks to Antony for having stopped a civil war before it could get started. Next they voted to thank Brutus and his fellow conspirators for what they had done. Then they shared out provinces: Brutus was given Crete, Cassius was given Africa.

Finally they discussed Caesar's will and the arrangements for his funeral. Antony and his supporters wanted the will to be read in public. They also demanded that he should not be buried privately but should have full honours – otherwise the common people would be angered. Cassius argued vehemently against this, but Brutus agreed to it.

He allowed Antony to take complete charge of Caesar's funeral. This was a fatal mistake.

V.12   The funeral of Caesar

Suet.
Caes. 84
The funeral was announced and a pyre was raised in the Field of Mars next to the tomb of Julia. On the rostra in the Forum they set up a golden shrine which was a model of the Temple of Mother Venus. Inside there was a couch of ivory with covers of crimson and gold. At its head stood a pillar over which were spread the clothes in which Caesar had been murdered. It was clear that one day would not be long enough for all those who wanted to bring gifts for the dead man, so the people were told to bring their gifts to the Field of Mars along any street they wanted, and not to bother about coming in order of rank.

At the funeral games words from plays were recited including this line:
Did I save these men so they could murder me?
This was to make the people pity Caesar and feel anger at his death.

Plut.
Brutus 20
Anthony 14
and Suet.
Caes. 84
When the people heard that he had left 75 drachmas to every single Roman and had given the people his gardens which lie across the Tiber they felt an amazing tenderness and their hearts ached for him.

Caesar's body was now carried out and Antony gave the usual speech in praise of the dead man. When he realised that the people were being deeply moved by his words, his praise for Caesar changed to pity for his death. As he finished speaking, he waved the dead man's clothes in the air, all stained with blood. He unfolded them so that everyone could see each gash and count the number of Caesar's wounds.

'The men who did this are the vilest murderers!' he shouted. At this the crowd lost all control of their emotions. Some shouted out 'Kill the murderers!' Others dragged benches and counters out of nearby shops and piled them up to make a huge pyre. On top they lifted Caesar's body and there, in a perfect setting amongst all the temples, sanctuaries and holy places, they set light to it. There were pipers and actors who had dressed up for the occasion in costumes which had been worn in Caesar's triumphs. Now they tore them off, ripped them to shreds and threw them into the fire.

Old soldiers who had fought with him threw the swords and armour which they had put on for the funeral into the fire. Many women threw in their jewels and their children's amulets and clothes. Crowds of foreigners, came to show their grief each according to their national custom. Then, when the flames were leaping high, people darted in from all sides to snatch up burning timbers and ran to the houses of the murderers to set them on fire. But Brutus and his friends were by now well barricaded in and managed to beat off the attack.

Plut.
Brutus 20 There was a man called Cinna, a poet. He had nothing to do with the murder at all – in fact he had been a friend of Caesar's. This man had a dream in which Caesar invited him to dinner, but he turned down the invitation. Caesar urged him to come and in the end took hold of his hand and led him hesitating and bewildered into a gloomy yawning place. After this Cinna fell into a fever which lasted all night. Next morning he was ashamed not to attend his friend's funeral and went out into the crowd when it had already become savage. Some of the crowd thought that he was the same Cinna who had spoken against Caesar at the assembly. 40 45

They tore him to pieces.

Epilogue

The conspirators do not seem to have formed any plans beyond the murder of Caesar. They presumably hoped that peace would return and with it the old republican government in its traditional form. They were wrong.

In 43 B.C. power was seized again by a group of three:

Mark Antony – former tribune of the people, and consul in 44 B.C. 5

Lepidus – Caesar's 'master of the horse'.

Octavian – Caesar's great nephew.

Octavian was only nineteen at the time, but Caesar had already noted his talent. In his will, Caesar adopted Octavian and made him his son and heir.

In the following year a great battle took place at Philippi in Greece, in which 10 Brutus and Cassius were defeated. Plutarch tells us that Brutus and Cassius committed suicide, Cassius using the dagger with which he had murdered Caesar. The three victors then split up the Roman world between them. Lepidus took control of Africa, but his influence declined and he was eventually forced to retire. Octavian received Italy and the West, where he dealt with any remaining 15 opposition. Antony took control of the East, but soon began to show more interest in Cleopatra than in Rome. In the end, he was defeated by Octavian at the battle of Actium, which took place off the shores of Greece in 31 B.C.

Unlike Caesar, Octavian managed to maintain his position of power. He did not become perpetual dictator and avoided any suspicion that he wanted to be a king. 20 Instead he claimed to have restored the Republic – but allowed himself to be granted several powers which had formerly been in the hands of different individuals. His prestige was acknowledged when he was granted the title 'Augustus' – the name by which he is known today.

In the Forum, Augustus built a temple to mark the spot where Caesar's body had 25 been cremated. In it he placed a painting of Venus and a statue of Divine Julius, with a comet emblazoned on his brow.

The Temple of Divine Julius, as it may once have looked and as it appears today. The recess between the steps is thought to mark the spot where Caesar's body was cremated.

'Make a star from the soul which was snatched from his murdered body, so that Divine Julius may forever look out upon our Capitol and Forum from his lofty temple'. (Ovid 43 B.C. – 17 A.D.)

Greek and Roman writers

Appian   lived during the second century A.D. He was born in Alexandria and moved to Rome where he was a lawyer. He wrote a history of Rome in Greek.

Caesar   As well as following the military and political career described in this book, Gaius Julius Caesar (about 100 B.C. – 44 B.C.) was well known as a public speaker and writer. His works include books about his campaigns in Gaul and his account of the civil war.

Lucan   Marcus Annaeus Lucanus was born in A.D. 39 and died in A.D. 65. Only a few lines of his many works survived except for the *Civil War* which is almost complete. It is an epic poem about the war between Caesar and Pompey.

Macrobius   Ambrosius Theodosius Macrobius lived in the early fifth century A.D. The *Saturnalia*, a miscellany of a wide range of topics, is his most substantial surviving work.

Plutarch   (born before A.D.50 and died after A.D.120) spent most of his life on the mainland of Greece and at Rome. He wrote many books including works of philosophy and a series of parallel biographies of famous Greeks and Romans.

Suetonius   Gaius Suetonius Tranquillus (born about A.D.70) spent most of his life in the imperial service. His main work is his *Lives of the Caesars*, biographies of Julius Caesar and the first eleven emperors from Augustus to Domitian. As secretary to the Emperor Hadrian, Suetonius had access to official records, but he also makes use of gossip and many other sources.